The Director and Don Juan

THE STORY SISTERS, BOOK #2
THE BLUEBERRY LANE SERIES

KATY REGNERY

Blueberry
LANE

THE DIRECTOR AND DON JUAN

This book is a work of fiction. Names, characters, places, and
incidents are products of the author's imagination or are used
fictitiously. Any resemblance to actual events, locales, or persons,
living or dead, is entirely coincidental.
Bahía de Plata is a fictional place.

Please visit my website at www.katyregnery.com
First Edition: June 2017
Katy Regnery
The Director and Don Juan: a novel / by Katy Regnery – 1st ed.
ISBN: 978-1-944810-14-6

The Blueberry Lane Series

THE ENGLISH BROTHERS
Breaking Up with Barrett
Falling for Fitz
Anyone but Alex
Seduced by Stratton
Wild about Weston
Kiss Me Kate
Marrying Mr. English

THE WINSLOW BROTHERS
Bidding on Brooks
Proposing to Preston
Crazy about Cameron
Campaigning for Christopher

THE ROUSSEAUS
Jonquils for Jax
Marry Me Mad
J.C. and the Bijoux Jolis

THE STORY SISTERS
The Bohemian and the Businessman
The Director and Don Juan
The Flirt and the Fox
The Saint and the Scoundrel

THE AMBLERS
Belonging to Bree
Surrendering to Sloane

THE ATWELLS
Four books to be named
Coming 2019

Muchas gracias a Jennifer Nieves, Linda Vega, Veronica Del Valle, y Wilmari Delgado.

You were my Puerto Rico experts and generously shared your cultural background and knowledge with me. I am so grateful to each of you, and I hope that Carlos makes you proud.
#MachoBoricua

CONTENTS

Prologue

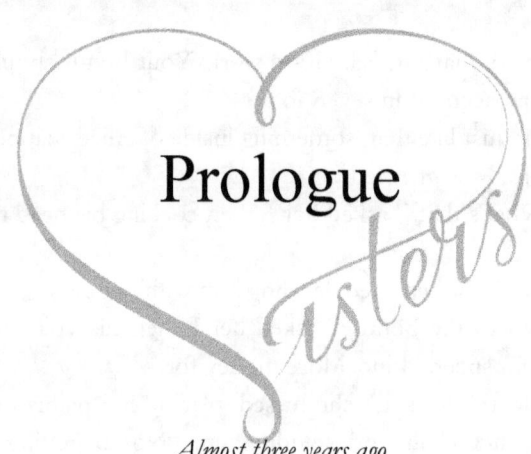

Almost three years ago

Alice Story seethed inside, barely hearing what her father was saying.

The gist of it was this: *You're an excellent employee. You're doing great work. I'm raising your salary and giving you a five-figure bonus, but you will not be promoted.* Again.

For five years, Alice Story had worked her ass off for her father's company, Story Imports. At her desk before anyone else arrived and staying long after everyone else had gone home, she was only outperformed occasionally by her father's lapdog, Shane Olson, who had been promoted four times in the five years that she and Shane had been working shoulder to shoulder on identical projects.

For some reason, Alice had convinced herself that this year—her fifth anniversary at Story Imports—her father would surprise her with a big promotion. As the eldest Story child, and after such intense dedication, she dreamed that she'd skip the title of manager and be promoted directly to vice president…or at least director.

Alas, no. Her title remained at associate, and she'd had it.

"…so, that's it, gal. Good work. Your bonus should hit your bank account in seven to ten—"

And just like that, something inside of Alice snapped.

"No," she growled.

"What's that?" asked her father, cocking his head to the side.

"No," she repeated, leveling him with her eyes.

"No to the bonus?" asked her father, his voice taking on a slight sneer. "Fine. More money for—"

"No to all of it," she hissed, placing her palms on the arms of her chair and standing up. "No to getting your coffee…No to staying here until midnight…No to coming in at five in the morning for conference calls to Paris and staying until after eight for conference calls to Napa…No to sitting in a cube when I deserve an office…No to the embarrassment of being your daughter and still being an associate. No, no, no, no, NO!" She balled up her hands and brought them down on his desk with a definitive thud. "No more!"

"You forget yourself, Alice Hughes Sto—"

"I *remember* myself, Father!" she bellowed, fury and injustice reddening her cheeks and fueling her tirade. "I *remember* that I went to Princeton undergrad. I *remember* that I went to the Wharton School of Business. I *remember* that I have been working here for five long, insufferable years!"

Her father leaped to his feet. "Get out! Get out of my office, you ungrateful—"

"*I* am ungrateful?" she shrieked, pounding the desk again. "*I* am ungrateful? I am responsible and dutiful and have given you *everything* I have inside my head and my heart since the day I graduated from business school! And yet you *refuse* to promote me. You *refuse* to let me rise up in this company that *my* grandfather Morrow started because you are a sexist, masochistic PIG!"

"GET OUT!" he half-growled, half-yelled, his face bright red and his eyeballs bulging from their sockets. "GET THE *HELL* OUT! You're *FIRED*!"

"Well, that's fine," she hissed, "because I QUIT!"

Turning her back on her father, she marched out of his office, hurling open the door, which slammed against the wall, the handle burying itself into the drywall with a loud and definitive crunch.

Standing before her, his hands on a rolling mailroom cart and his gray eyes wide as saucers, was…was…the guy from the mail room. He stared at her unblinkingly, which clued Alice into the fact that the entire office had just heard every word of her dramatic resignation. Holding his gaze, which felt—for no good reason—like the peaceful eye of a brutal, unforgiving storm, she clenched her jaw once and took a shaky breath through her teeth.

"You've got this," he whispered in Spanish-accented English, nodding slowly, deep dimples denting his brown cheeks as he pursed his full lips.

Still staring into his clear gray eyes, she nodded back, spying her cubicle desk behind him. "Yes, I do."

Brushing his shoulder as she stepped forward, she knelt on the desk, placing one heeled shoe flat on the surface next to her keyboard, then the other. Standing to her full height so that she could see over the tops of the twenty or so cubicles on the office floor, she loosened her jaw and took a deep, cleansing breath.

Looking down at—Juan? Julio?—once more for support, she raised her chin and cleared her throat.

"Fellow employees!"

The office was already fairly quiet, most of the personnel having heard the fight she had with her father and stopping to gawk. Now they looked up at her in shock, staring at the boss's daughter standing on top of her desk.

"Do any of you value your dignity? Do any of you want to get ahead at a company where you will be judged on your contributions, not your gender or race? Do any of you feel passed over for advancement here because you're not kissing my father's ass?"

She glanced down at the mail room guy again, pausing for a millisecond to realize that his eyelashes were obscenely long and curled up at the end. He blinked up at her, and she shook her head to clear it, looking out at the sea of stunned eyes staring back at her.

"I'm starting a new company! And it's called...um, *Alice* Story Imports! *All of you* are welcome to come and work for me!"

***

Carlos Vega stared up at Alice Story as she made her impetuous offer to the employees of her father's company.

He'd heard Alice and her father screaming at each other, of course—everyone in Philadelphia had probably heard them—but he'd never seen anything quite as glorious, or half as brave, as Alice Story standing on a desk, telling her father, in so many words, to go straight to hell.

Carlos, who'd started in the Story Imports mail room just over eight months ago after earning his bachelor's degree in business administration, had hoped to rise more quickly through the ranks of the company. But taking one look at the very white management told him that it would be an uphill, possibly impossible battle for a Hispanic man.

Still, he'd worked hard and hoped that one day he'd have an opportunity to move from mail room coordinator to corporate associate. Unlikely? Maybe. But Carlos was a dreamer, and he knew that if someone would give him a chance, he could prove his worth.

Looking up at Alice Story, who waited for someone—*anyone*—to take her up on her offer, it occurred to him that this, *here and now*, was his chance.

Though Alice lived and worked—and, hell, *breathed*—in a stratosphere way above a man who'd grown up on the tiny island of Puerto Rico, sharing a respectable but very modest home with three generations of Vegas, he knew that her offer was made from the heart. She had experienced discrimination at the hands of her father; she wasn't likely to perpetuate it within her own company.

"Me," he heard himself whisper.

Alice looked down at him, shock written across her face. "Did you say something?"

"Uh." He cleared his throat. "*Me*. I would like to work for you."

His accent was stronger for his nerves, but his words were clear and decisive, and Alice's lips twitched in relief as she jerked a nod at him. "What's your name?"

"Carlos, Miss Alice."

"Carlos," she said. "That's 'Charles,' right?"

Hearing her say his name made something inside of him clench tightly, then release, and he had a vague thought that hearing San Pedro call your name at the pearly gates would have nothing on Alice Story translating it from Spanish to English.

"*Sí, lo es,*" he murmured in Spanish, then quickly switched to English. "Uh. Yes. That's right."

"Thank you, Charles," she whispered. "You won't regret it." She raised her chin, put her hands on her hips, and called out over the heads of her erstwhile coworkers, "Is anyone else interested in a fresh start away from this hellhole?"

Somewhere across the office, a paper clip dropped to the floor, an isolated sound in the thick silence.

Behind him, Mr. Story's office door opened, and Carlos turned to find his boss standing in the doorway, his face twisted with fury and disdain.

"Security's on their way up, gal," he sneered. "Get out and good riddance!"

He slammed his door, which reverberated around the silent, still office, every employee transfixed on the drama that had just unfolded before them. But then a phone rang, and the entire office got back to work, humming with the sound of employees going about their usual business.

Carlos turned back to Alice, watching as she flinched, her brows kitting together in disbelief as she realized that no one else at Story Imports was willing to take a chance on her.

"Miss Alice," he said, "are you okay?"

She looked down at him, her eyes slightly glassy. "Yes."

"I meant it. I will work for you."

"Alice."

"What?"

"Just call me Alice." Her lips twitched briefly as she sized him up. For a moment, he thought—hoped—she might smile at him, but she didn't. She raised her chin instead. "I promise…you won't regret it."

He let his hand slip from the mesh basket he'd been pushing around the office and raised it to her. "I trust you."

Glancing down at his hand for a long moment, she finally took it, holding onto him as she lowered herself to her knees, then climbed off the desk. The office around them buzzed with normal activity as though nothing out of the ordinary had just taken place.

She let go of his hand, took a framed photo of herself and her four sisters off the desk, and shoved it into her purse. Then she said, "I've got everything I need. Ready to go?"

"Yes, ma'am." He nodded. "Alice."

As she turned and left her cubicle—her posture perfect as she walked down the hallway, past the conference room, past the reception desk, to the elevator lobby—her choppy and shallow breathing was the only indication she was rattled.

When they reached the elevator bank, Carlos hit the call button, then turned to Alice, who just stared at the double doors in silence. When the doors dinged open, he stepped onto the elevator beside his new boss, watching the chrome doors close in front of them and hoping like hell that he'd made the right decision.

Chapter 1

Present Day

Buzz. Buzz. Buzz. Buzz.

Pause.

Buzz. Buzz. Buzz. Buzz.

Carlos drew his arm from beneath the warm sheets and reached for his phone, fumbling for the snooze button.

Buzz. Buzz—

Ahhhh. Silence.

It seemed like seconds after he slipped back to sleep that his cell phone buzzed again, but this time, a woman's voice added to the noise unexpectedly with a low-toned *"Ay, Dios! Cállate!"*

Shocked to discover he had company, Carlos' eyes popped open as he hit snooze again. Scrambling to remember who was in bed with him and coming up blank, he shifted slowly, turning his body to look at her. Lying on her back beside him with a tangled mess of black hair on his pillow and her face smeared with last night's makeup was…was…hmm.

Alicia?

Felicia?

He turned away from her, rubbing his face as he sat up. Fuck. He had a vague recollection of dancing with her at Tierra last night toward the end of the *fiesta*. She was—his brain wasn't firing quickly this morning—his cousin Lena's friend? Right?

He sighed, placing a hand on her bare shoulder and shaking her gently. "Uh…you gotta go, *mami*. It's morning."

"*Me voy a dormir*," she answered drowsily. *I'm going back to sleep.*

He shook her shoulder a little harder. "Listen, I'm sorry, but you gotta go. It's Monday. I've got work. I've gotta shower." She didn't move, so he spoke a little louder. "*Mira, chula*, my boss is no nonsense. I can't be late."

"He sounds like an asshole," she muttered into the pillow.

She, actually.

Alice.

He ground his jaw, bristling at the dirtiness of the word *asshole* used anywhere near her name or person.

His voice was cooler when he spoke again. "Not at all. Just expects me to be on time. So *you* gotta go."

Opening her eyes and lowering the sheet to uncover perfect tan breasts with chocolate-colored nipples, she pouted. "What If I'm not ready to go yet, *papi*? What if I want to stay a little longer?"

His eyes rested on her tits for a only a moment before he shook his head and turned away, sweeping the covers from his naked body and swinging his legs over the side of the bed. He stood up with his back to her, stretched his arms over his head, flexed his ass, then leaned down and picked up her hot-pink panties from the floor. Looking at her over his shoulder, he threw them onto the bed beside her.

"Don't matter what you want. I gotta shower. You gotta go. Don't play games."

Her eyes narrowed. "I don't remember you rushing me last night when I was sucking your cock."

Fuck, she was crass.

He exhaled deeply.

"And I don't remember promising you anything, *mami*." Why couldn't she just go already? He didn't want to be *un cabrón*, but she was starting to get on his nerves. Grabbing her matching bra from his closet door handle, he tossed it to her, adding some steel to his voice: "Party's over. You gotta get dressed and get out."

Her face changed from pissy to furious in an instant as she sat up, gathering her underwear onto her lap.

"*Pendejo*," she hissed, jamming her arms into her bra. She whipped her hair over her shoulder as she fastened the clasps in the back. "I'm telling Lena that you're an asshole."

He sighed inwardly. This was a hell of a way to start a Monday.

"Ain't nothing she don't already know," he said mildly, opening the bathroom door, then turning to face her over his shoulder. "Don't be mad. It was fun, okay?"

"Fuck you!" she cried, throwing something against the door just as he pulled it shut and locked it.

A shoe? Her purse? Could have been either. Didn't matter. He'd touch up the paint tonight. He couldn't waste any more time on last night's diversions. It was already seven ten, and Alice would expect him to be seated at his desk at eight o'clock sharp, her hot coffee and a list of today's appointments printed out and waiting on her blotter.

He took a piss, thankful to see a used condom in the toilet.

Carlos liked sex as much as any other hot-blooded

twentysomething, but he didn't especially want his cock to fall off from some sick disease, so he was always careful, no matter how much he'd had to drink.

"...*de puta*! You're a motherfucking pig!" yelled Alicia or Felicia through the door, finishing off an impressive string of insults. A moment later, he heard the angry clacking of her high heels across the parquet floor of his bedroom, and a second after that, his apartment door slammed shut.

"Thank fuck."

Breathing a sigh of relief, he flushed, then stepped over to the countertop, resting his hands on the edge of the sink and staring at himself in the mirror.

"You're getting too old for this shit, *papi*," he told his twenty-six-year-old reflection. Large gray eyes with crazy-long eyelashes in a perpetually tanned face looked back at him. Toned arms and contoured abs spoke to hours at the gym. *Good-looking motherfucker.* He grinned at himself, his dimples deepening as he shook his head. "But you're a fool too."

His smile faded as the words left his mouth, and he turned around, reached into the shower, and turned on the hot water. His *prima*, Lena, wasn't going to be thrilled with him when she found out he'd dogged her friend. Her parents were surrogate parents to Carlos here in Philadelphia, and if Alicia—Felicia?—went whining to them, he'd certainly get a text later today about his behavior.

Piensa que eres un Don Juan, pero eres un pendejo sinvergüenza. (*You think you're Don Juan, but you're a shameless idiot.*)

He could hear Tia Carmen's sharp disapproval echo in his head.

Por qué haces eso? No eres basura! (*Why do you do this? You aren't trash!*)

That would come from his uncle, who was his mother's

older brother. And shit, he wouldn't relish it, because his uncle's opinion meant something to him. He wasn't eager to disappoint him, nor did he want to embarrass his family in the large but surprisingly intimate community of *Centro de Oro*, the epicenter of the Puerto Rican population in Philly. And he knew that playing fast and loose with the daughters of their friends was something they didn't condone.

Alicia-Felicia had put out last night, yes, but if she was Lena's friend, she was probably a semidecent girl from a semidecent family, since Lena didn't hang out with garbage. Which meant that Lena had probably vouched for him as her cousin. So by fucking Felicia-Alicia last night and kicking her out of his place this morning without making future plans to see her again he'd acted ungallantly.

"You need to make some changes, bro," he muttered to himself as he squirted shampoo into his hand and rubbed it through his close-cropped, slightly kinky black hair. Tuning around, he let the water sluice down has back, carrying the suds down the drain. *You gotta change your ways, papi. No comas donde cagas.*

Or, in other words, *Don't shit where you eat.*

Grabbing a bottle of shower gel, he squeezed some into his palm and rubbed his hands together before sliding them over the ripples of muscle on his chest, then down over his dick, which stirred to life from the attention.

"No more one-night stands," he muttered, annoyed with himself, removing his hands from his semi to rinse his body and turn off the water. He didn't have time to jerk off this morning, and besides, he didn't deserve the pleasure.

He grabbed a fluffy snow-white towel from the shelf beside the toilet and wrapped it around his waist, rubbing the mirror with the side of his hand.

When he arrived in the states seven years ago after

graduating from the *Universidad Interamericana de Puerto Rico* with a degree in business administration, he'd moved directly from his parent's house in Toa Baja to his aunt and uncle's place in Fairhill, Philadelphia. At first he had worked odd jobs while looking for a corporate job in the city until he found a position as mail room coordinator at Story Imports.

It wasn't a job he'd wanted. Carlos didn't mind paying his dues, but after achieving a bachelor's degree, he'd hoped for a better entry-level position. He couldn't help but feel that his race had affected his prospects, consigning him to the mail room regardless of his education.

Leaving Story Imports to work for Alice was the best move he'd ever made. Though Alice Story Imports had struggled for the first year or so, after Alice's sister Priscilla got married two years ago, she made a substantial investment of capital into the company, and everything had quickly changed.

True to her original promise, Alice had raised his salary and promoted him to office manager right away, and he'd finally started making enough money to move out of his uncle's house and find his own place: a hip, two-story loft, about a fifteen-minute walk from *Centro de Oro*.

Carlos had reveled in his newfound freedom. After twenty-five years of sharing a bedroom with his brothers in Toa Baja or his cousin Enrique here in Philly? Having his own space was heaven.

And heaven sure included a lot of angels.

It was just so *easy*.

So goddamned easy to meet someone at a club and invite her back to his place, where they had the privacy to do whatever they wanted. No risk of his parents, grandmother, siblings, nephews, aunt, uncle, or cousins walking in. No need to drive to a secluded place, where he might get busted for indecent exposure. No need to find a cheap motel room where bed bugs were likely and romance was null.

Suddenly, he had a place of his own where he could invite anyone. And so, for two years, he'd whored his way through Philly, fucking whenever and whomever he pleased, without commitment, without guilt, and—most of the time—without a second thought. He was finally his own boss. And yeah, it was fun.

Except lately…it wasn't.

Lately it felt like a drag. He didn't feel like romancing some anonymous woman the next day. He didn't feel like being charming and asking her out on a proper date the following weekend. He just wanted her to get out. And it's not that it felt dirty or bad, because sex was sex, and it *always* felt good…but lately he wanted—fuck, what did he want?

More.

When he looked at Lena's brother, his cousin Diego, holding his new baby with his arm around his pretty wife, Luz, something inside of Carlos clenched with longing. Family was important to him. *Really* important. Unlike his American counterparts, who seemed to put off fatherhood for as long as possible, Carlos had always imagined himself having two or three kids before he was thirty. Here he was, already twenty-six, and still playing the field like a *cabrón*.

Maybe it was time to get serious, find the right girl, and settle down. Someone to keep him in line. Someone whom he could see as the mother of his kids. Someone he wouldn't dream of kicking out of bed because all he'd want is for her to stay.

Yeah. *Stay.* Forever.

A face flashed through his mind at the thought of forever and he winced, frowning at himself. The one girl—the only *woman*—he really wanted was so far out of his league, so far above and beyond him, he forced her face away. No point in pining for the impossible. There were plenty of nice girls he could meet through Lena or Luz. Girls who'd see him as a catch, as "forever" material.

Finishing a quick shave and patting his cheeks with aftershave, he whipped off the towel and padded back into his room naked. Choosing a crisp white dress shirt and gray suit from his closet, he got dressed, removing his St. Christopher medal, which he only wore on weekends.

Checking out his reflection in the full-length mirror, he decided he looked good enough for a Monday and started to close the closet door, then stopped.

You want more? he thought. *Start acting like it.*

"For starters, no more nights like last night. And no more…" He sighed, annoyed with himself as the words trailed off. Grimacing at his reflection, he closed the closet door and headed down the stairs.

…wanting what you absolutely cannot have.

***

Across town, Alice Story glanced at the timer on her bedroom treadmill, swiping the sweat from her forehead with the back of her hand. In front of her, she had CNBC on mute, the ticker tape of letters and numbers sliding smoothly, comfortingly, across the bottom of the TV screen. The world was awake and working, and Alice, who'd started her own company three years ago, was a part of it—a part that she would have been denied had she remained working for her father.

Her father, with whom she hadn't spoken in three years. Not since the Sunday supper her sister Priscilla had hosted to announce her marriage and pregnancy.

Not that he'd reached out.

Not that she had either.

They may as well be dead to one another, and sad though it was, Alice found she could live with that.

As a child, Alice had sensed her father's disappointment that she wasn't a boy, and she'd worked hard to be the son he'd never had. She'd excelled in everything she tried: academics, tennis, golf, and lacrosse. She was the first violin in her prep school's orchestra and was accepted early admission to Princeton. There were no "wild oats" sowed in college, where she kept her reputation spic and span, thus ensuring the respectability of her family's name. She graduated Phi Beta Kappa and enrolled in the Wharton School of Business immediately, earning her MBA with honors and starting work at Story Imports the Monday after she matriculated. She accepted an associate-level position from her father, eager to start at the bottom of the corporate ladder and work her way up.

To her everlasting shame, she had still been under the illusion that if she did everything right—excelled in her grades and extracurricular activities, attended the right schools, and made her parents proud—she would one day take over the family business.

But years passed. One, then two. Then three. Then four. Her framed diplomas, on the wall of her home office, grew dusty, waiting for the chance to hang on the walls of what should be her office at Story Imports. But there was no promotion, no executive office, and the cube outside of her father's office became her own little prison as she realized that there would never be advancement—that all her hard work would *not* be rewarded with more responsibility. And on the rare occasions that she'd confronted her father, his response was that he'd never promised her anything.

Alice grew brittle in that little cube, corralled and conditioned like a veal for one humiliating purpose: to marry a respectable businessman who could run Story Imports *for* her.

But one morning, thank God, she'd found her voice again. Thirty-year-old Alice, who'd done everything right and had nothing to show for it, stood on a desk and told her father, in no uncertain terms, to go to hell, taking back the reins of her life and setting forth to build her own future.

The first year of Alice Story Imports had been difficult, fraught with challenges, mostly financial, that her trust-fund allowance could barely cover. Her family name had helped her obtain a loan, but the interest levels were high since it was mostly unsecured—her trust wouldn't be freely available to her for a decade. Just when she feared that she might have to throw in the towel, her sister Priscilla had announced her marriage to Shane Olson. Shane, as fed up as Alice with her father's underhanded ways, had come to work for her, and Priscilla's trust had provided a cash infusion that had given new life to the company—and a new name: Story Sisters Trading Ltd.

Since then? Alice had been sitting pretty. She worked hard to grown her business, but she was no longer worried about its longevity. She and Priscilla would have something solid and strong to pass on to their daughters one day, a fact that made Alice feel very proud.

Well, mostly proud.

Maybe a little wistful too.

Alice's younger sisters Margaret and Priscilla were both mothers, and Priscilla had just had her second child, a baby boy, in June. At thirty-three, Alice had no children, no husband, not even a boyfriend. How could she? She'd spent the last four years birthing a company from nothing. She hadn't had a moment to spare for a personal life of any kind; hell, the only human being she'd even seen with marked regularity over the past few years was her employee Carlos.

Alice felt her face soften at the thought of his huge gray eyes.

Carlos, who had followed her out the doors of Story Imports in her disastrous bid to poach her father's staff, would never know what it had meant to Alice to be trusted with his future. To her dying day, she would hold him in such high esteem; it would be hard for another employee to ever capture her devotion as he had.

That said, however, it wasn't like Alice had ever thought of Carlos in any capacity except as her employee. She would never consider dating someone who worked for her. No way. No how. Not in a million years. Her father had exercised unethical workplace habits, and Alice would not, under any circumstances, follow in his unsavory footsteps. Everything—*Every. Little. Thing.*—at SST would be kept fair, principled, and scrupulously ethical, no matter what.

Which meant that the only man she'd spent any time with over the past four years was absolutely, positively not a contender for her affection…and she definitely needed to get out more. Maybe now that SST was on firmer ground, she could start dating if she wanted to. Dating. Ugh. She couldn't think of anything that sounded less appealing. The entire process of dating had never come easily to Alice, who'd never sustained a relationship for longer than a month or two.

But your eggs aren't getting any younger, she thought ruefully.

And unlike some other successful businesswomen she knew, she refused to consider having a child on her own via a donor. She wanted her kids to have the loving mother and father that she and her sisters had never experienced. It was just so goddamn daunting to consider the process of getting there: meeting someone, clicking with them, establishing intimacy, falling in love, planning a wedding, and finally—years down the road—getting pregnant. It made her head spin to even consider it.

Strapped to the console on the treadmill, her mobile phone buzzed, and she looked down at the screen to see that Margaret was calling. Alice plugged in her earbuds without breaking stride and pressed answer.

"Megs?"

"Good morning!"

"Good morning," said Alice. "What's up?"

"Just wanted to thank you for coming yesterday…and for getting the gift. I think Pris loved it."

Over the weekend, Margaret had hosted a sisters-only "Welcome Baby" luncheon at her winery for Priscilla, who had given birth to baby Theodore the first weekend in June. For a gift, Alice, Margaret, and Jane had all chipped in and purchased an original Edgar Alwin Payne landscape of New Mexico for baby Theo's Santa Fe–inspired nursery. At a contribution of $20,000 each, it was an extravagant gift that Alice had tracked down through Libitz Feingold Rousseau's gallery in New York, but the look on Priscilla's face—and her deluge of tears and shrieks—was priceless.

"She did. My ears are still ringing from all her shouting; how did the baby sleep through it?"

Margaret laughed good-naturedly. "Thanks for all the footwork—finding it and getting it here."

"No problem. How are *you* feeling?"

Margaret, who had one child—Ogden—with her husband, Cameron Winslow, had announced yesterday that she was ten weeks pregnant with their second child.

"Like I want to throw up every ten minutes," groaned Margaret.

"That'll go away soon, won't it?" asked Alice, her

knowledge of pregnancy thin.

"By sixteen weeks, hopefully," she said. "I've still got a little while of feeling cheerfully miserable."

The pragmatic side of Alice wanted to say, *Well, you're the one who got pregnant. Suck it up.* But she was trying to better calibrate her responses to her sisters lately, so she scrambled to think of something more comforting. *Hmm. What is comforting? Oh. Tea. Tea is always a good idea, right?*

"Maybe a cup of tea would help."

Margaret's voice was warm. "Right. Thanks, Alice."

Vaguely uncomfortable that she was older than Margaret yet had no solid advice to offer, she shifted gears. "Sorry Bets wasn't there. She's an ass."

"You tried."

Their sister Elizabeth had not attended the luncheon. Over the past three years, she'd become closer and closer to their father, until the two were practically joined at the hip, living together at Forrester and working together at Story Imports.

Elizabeth objected greatly to the fact that Alice, Margaret, and Priscilla had all worked for Story Imports, then quit, turning their proverbial backs on their father and supporting Alice's competing business. Still, Elizabeth was their sister, and Alice had invited her to Priscilla's shower via e-mail, urging her to attend. Elizabeth had politely declined, saying that celebrating Priscilla with Alice at Margaret's vineyard would upset their father.

"Hey, Alice…" said Margaret softly, like she was backing into a conversation topic.

"Hmm?"

"Are you…I mean, I was just wondering if…well, if you're seeing anyone?"

She frowned. "For what?"

"Um…no, I don't mean a doctor or specialist. I mean…a man. You know…a *boyfriend*," said Margaret, her voice mildly exasperated. She hurried to add, "I mean, you've always sort of kept your private life, well, private. But…I don't know. Pris and I are having kids, and Jane's dating someone on the sly. Bets is the worst flirt I ever met, so I'm positive she's stringing some poor slob along, but you…"

"I've been a little busy the past couple of years."

"I've noticed," said Margaret, "but…you've got everything now. An amazing company that you own, a gorgeous apartment, sisters who love you, money in the bank…don't you want someone special too? Someone to share it all with?"

"Sure," she said, pressing the stop button on the treadmill. "Eventually."

She picked up the remote control and switched off the TV. Her large, elegant, cream-colored bedroom was bathed in soft morning light, which streamed through French doors to gild the gold handpulls of her dresser drawers and the two lamps on either side of her king-sized bed. She stood in the golden light for a moment, considering her sister's question, uncertain if her cheeks were hot from exercise or from the awkward turn in the conversation.

"Well…?" prompted Margaret.

"Well what?"

"Do you…I mean, are you seeing anyone?"

"No."

A couple of times a year, she might meet a man—either via business or on her travels—with whom she connected. She didn't sleep with most of them; Alice wasn't easy, but when she did engage in an affair, she made every effort to be certain the liaison was discreet.

Margaret cleared her throat. "Cameron has so many

friends. Would you like to, you know, be set up?"

"You mean…on a blind date?"

"It could be more casual than that!" Margaret insisted. "We could host a party…point out a few eligible bachelors…"

"A party for me to find a boyfriend?"

"Do you hate the idea?"

Strangely enough, she didn't. It made a certain amount of sense to let her respectably married sister help her find a mate. It wasn't very sexy or romantic, but it appealed to Alice's pragmatic sensibilities. She just wanted to think it over before saying yes.

"It's time for work," she said, plucking her phone from the console and heading for the shower.

"It's always time for work," said Margaret softly. "What do you say? About the party?"

"I'll get back to you."

"You'll think about it?" asked Margaret, a surprised lift in her voice.

"I will," said Alice. "I have to go now. Have a good day. Try some tea."

"Will do," said her sister. "Bye, Alice."

"Bye."

She turned on the shower, took out the earbuds, laid them on her bathroom counter, and looked at her red, sweating face in the mirror.

Don't you want someone special?

She sighed deeply at her reflection. Of course she did.

She just feared that what she wanted didn't exist.

Someone who would respect and support her business goals but still treat her like a woman. Someone who would understand her but still challenge her. Someone she could admire for his own drive and ambition but who wouldn't expect for her to give up her professional objectives in order to requite her personal dreams. Someone who might defy traditional gender roles and take charge of their home and care for their children. Or at least share those responsibilities with her. Neither a tyrant nor a fool, Alice wanted a *teammate* in every sense of the word. And though she often doubted such a man existed, she couldn't deny that she hoped he did.

So...yes, she decided grudgingly, shrugging out of her sweaty workout clothes as she stepped into the steamy shower. She'd call Margaret later and accept her offer.

At this point, she had nothing to lose.

Chapter 2

Carlos unlocked the glass doors to the offices of Story Sisters Trading Ltd. and flicked on the reception-area lights, circling the modern-style chrome desk and opening another glass door that led down a narrow hallway. Pictures of vineyards in California, South Africa, Australia, and Argentina adorned the crisp white walls as his loafers padded on the thick gray carpet. He walked past the small lime-colored conference room, stopped in the pantry quickly, then continued by the copy machine and file room to enter the main part of the office. Appreciating the quiet of the empty space, he took a moment to relish the silence before turning on the overhead lights, which came to life with a hum.

Against the exterior wall straight ahead of him were four glass offices: Alice's, the largest, to the far left, was directly in front of him. To the right of hers was the office of Shane Olson, the vice president of sales, and to the right of his, two additional offices remained empty, ready for the vice presidents that Alice intended to hire over the course of the next two years.

Outside of the offices, in the area where Carlos now

stood, were ten large cubicles and an open-plan conference/meeting/brainstorming table and whiteboard for the manager and associate-level employees. Carlos beelined for his desk, located just outside of Alice's office, and placed his laptop bag on the desk chair, the keys in his hand jingling as he reached forward to turn on his computer screen.

Plucking her venti cold brew from a cardboard tray in his other hand, Carlos unlocked Alice's office door and turned on the lights, setting her coffee beside her keyboard and powering on her computer. Finding the TV remote where she'd left it last night—on the Plexiglas coffee table in front of a lime-green leather sofa—he tuned the television to CNBC, muting the sound before placing the remote on her desk beside her keyboard. From his pocket, he pulled the KIND granola bar—dark-chocolate cherry, her favorite—he'd grabbed from the pantry and placed it beside her cup of coffee. Then he stretched his arms over his head and yawned as he walked over to the windows that looked out over the City of Brotherly Love.

When Priscilla had invested in SST two years ago, Alice had moved their small company to these newer, brighter, much posher offices in a downtown high-rise building. Carlos had sat in on every meeting with the realtor and architects, taking notes for Alice so she could be hands-free to discuss her plans and negotiate contracts. More than anything else, she'd insisted that her staff enjoy the same view that she did. She'd been express in her wishes that the executive offices were bright and open, with glass walls that allowed natural light to filter through the windows to the administrative and associate staff cubes on the main floor.

Carlos marveled at the view from her floor-to-ceiling windows for a moment as he did every morning, remembering the office that had come before.

He and Alice had sat back-to-back at identical secondhand desks with identical secondhand chairs that squealed when they rolled across the floor. It was a one-room office with only three hundred square feet of space and barely enough room to move around. Still, they'd made it work…and in that small, intimate space, Carlos had gotten to know his boss very well.

You'd never know it from her stern demeanor and frank-speaking ways, but Alice Story had a heart as big as the ocean, and she'd been that way for as long as he'd known her, quietly and without any expectation of praise doing what was right, not just for herself, but for everyone.

She offered her employees top-of-the-line health care; four-month maternity and paternity leave; a minimum of three weeks paid vacation for all employees, even those at the administrative level; and most important of all, tuition reimbursement for any employee who had worked at SST for a minimum of three years, a short list that currently only included Carlos.

Turning back to his cube, Carlos picked up his own hot, full-octane coffee, taking a sip as he moved his laptop bag to the floor and sat down in his desk chair. Thinking, as he often did lately, about Alice's tuition reimbursement policy, he opened the bottom drawer of his desk and stared for a moment at the completed application for admission at the Wharton School of Business at the University of Pennsylvania. He'd filled it out two months ago, asking Shane, in strictest confidence, to write him a recommendation. Shane had written a monumental letter too, but Carlos still feared that his undergraduate education, at a Puerto Rican university, wouldn't be good enough for the Wharton admissions board.

He closed the drawer.

He was probably best off where he was.

Even after they moved to these offices, Alice had kept him beside her as her "Guy Friday" and right-hand man. She'd also promoted him to office manager, which meant that in addition to helping Alice, Carlos was responsible for the hiring and firing all support staff, supply procurement, building management, office contracts, and matters of real estate.

And lately, because Shane didn't speak a lick of Spanish and Alice was interested in importing more South American wines, he was acting as a translator for their sales force.

All around, it was a good job—respectable and multifaceted—and Alice paid very well. Leaving to go to business school didn't really make a lot of sense. Or so he told himself. In quiet moments, when he allowed his heart to dream, to tell him what it wanted most of all, his reasons for staying exactly where he was took on a much more personal focus. Maybe what it really boiled down to was that he didn't want to leave *her*.

"Hi, Carlos," said a woman's voice, and he looked up to see Shane's assistant, Gloria, standing over his desk.

"Morning, Gloria."

She grinned at him, eyes sparkling as she moaned, "You're lookin' *fiiiine* this morning, *papi*."

Like him, Gloria was part of the large Puerto Rican population in Philadelphia, though unlike him, she'd been born here in the States.

He adopted the sort of no-nonsense expression he'd learned from Alice. "Let's go easy on the slang today, okay? You know better."

Gloria pursed her red lips and arched her back so her tits stuck out. "You're not better than me."

"I never said I was, Gloria. But that's not an

appropriate comment to make to your supervisor. If I said the same to you, I could be suspended for harassment."

"I was giving you a compliment, Carlos."

He wasn't going to let her get away with it. "Would you give Miss Story the same compliment? Would you tell her, 'You're lookin' *fiiiiiine* this morning, *mami*'?"

"N-No," she sputtered, dropping his eyes, her cheeks flushing with color.

He didn't meant to embarrass her, but Gloria was younger than he was by several years, and she'd only been working at SST for a few weeks. And he knew Alice. If she ever heard Gloria saying something that overt and suggestive, Alice would ask for her dismissal. His boss was fair, but she ran a tight ship. It was better that Gloria learned it from him rather than ending up losing her job.

"No big deal, huh? Just, you know, be professional," he added to soften the blow of his words.

She looked up and nodded, giving him a small smile. "Shane asked me to remind you…even though he's coming back to work this week, he doesn't want to travel until his paternity leave is up."

When Priscilla gave birth two months ago, Shane had decided to take off eight weeks to help Priscilla with their daughter, Kaitlyn. He was entitled to eight more weeks of leave, but he'd agreed to work three days a week starting in August as long as he didn't have to travel until the sixteen weeks was up.

Carlos turned to his keyboard, accessing Alice's calendar and taking a look at it. "She doesn't have any scheduled trips coming up…but I'll remind her just to be safe."

"Morning, Carlos! Gloria!"

A group of three associates on Shane's team turned the

corner, passing by Carlos' desk, and he nodded hello to them.

As Gloria slipped away with a little wave, Linda from accounts receivable stopped by his desk. "We're out of eight-and-a-half-by-fourteen paper."

"Linda, I got you six reams"—he reached for a stack of invoices in a plastic tray on his desk, flipping to the one he was looking for—"in June."

"I know." She shrugged. "But we're bigger now. Sorry. I need more to run the reports."

"Can you try to requisition it before you run out next time? It's cheaper for me to buy a whole case than a single ream."

"Sure thing," she said, nodding at him before she headed back to her office.

"Poland Springs is here," said Susan, the new receptionist, stopping by his desk with an invoice. "They've got three large water bot—"

"They go in the pantry," said Carlos. "Back left corner. You can sign for them."

"Great. Thanks," said Susan, hurrying back to the entry lobby.

Turning back to his computer, he looked at Alice's appointments for the day, noting an hour blocked off from nine until ten. He didn't recall who was coming in, so he clicked on the highlighted appointment, waiting for it to come up as he took another sip of coffee.

Eduardo Ramirez, Castillo Brothers Ltd. (Board of Directors)

Hmm. The meeting had been booked by Shane, not Alice.

Although Castillo Brothers Ltd. was a familiar name to Carlos—the company was started by three brothers about fifty years ago in Puerto Rico and had been, at one time, a competitor of the now much larger Bacardi—Ramirez was not.

Carlos didn't mind if Alice went into meetings blind as long as *he* had a firm grip on the sort of person with whom she was dealing. She was more than capable of handling whatever business came her way, of course, but more than once, Carlos had noted that some men wanted more from Alice than a good deal on exports.

Alice was beautiful, successful, ambitious, and clever.

She was also filthy rich. Or she would be. One day.

And Carlos had seen more than one fortune hunter try to get into her pants over the years. He much preferred to know *exactly* who she was dealing with so that he could run interference if necessary. If Shane booked the meeting, the guy was probably legit business-wise, but that really wasn't Carlos' primary concern. He wanted to know what *kind* of man he was.

Glancing around his shoulder to be sure Alice wasn't walking in, Carlos opened an Internet browser to do a little background check on Ramirez's personal life before she arrived.

A moment later, he stared at a picture of bronzed, blue-eyed Eduardo Ramirez, checking out his online resume.

Born in 1965, he was fifty-two years old but looked closer to forty, with salt-and-pepper hair, expensive glasses, cheerful creases around his eyes, and an overconfident smirk. Carlos raised his eyebrow as he noted that Ramirez was from Guaynabo, not far from the small Puerto Rican town where Carlos had been raised. Well, close in distance, perhaps, but actually worlds apart. Ramirez had been born into a lot of money. Back in the 1980s, a Puerto Rican didn't get *Harvard '86* and *Wharton '89* beside his name unless he'd come from some considerable wealth. And hired by a hedge fund straight out of Wharton? Oh, yeah. This guy was swimming in dough.

Opening a new tab on his browser, he surfed "Ramirez" again, adding the words "wife" and "girlfriend" to his search, and discovered that he'd been married and divorced not once, not twice, but three times. He had two children with wife number one, to whom he'd been married for seventeen years, and none with the latter two. Carlos' lips twitched as he noted the name of Ramirez's most recent wife, Gianna Maria Ramirez, which he entered into Facebook.

It didn't take long for him to find her—her picture showed a very tanned, blonde, thirtysomething woman wearing a sarong and pricey sunglasses on the beach with the bright-blue ocean in the background. Pretty in a *Real Housewives of Malibu* sort of way, she listed her current city as San Juan but noted that she was originally from Milan. A quick check of her public photo gallery resulted in a picture of Mrs. Ramirez from six years ago, when she was still Signorina Bianchi, wearing an Alitalia flight attendant uniform.

Carlos added and subtracted years, inserting the missing pieces quickly: Ramirez was still married to his second wife when he met Gianna Maria and hadn't been able to keep it in his pants. So he'd divorced wifey *numero dos* for Miss Mile High and married her...though the happy couple had only *remained* happy for a few years. After a massive wedding and three years of couple-selfies that were increasingly less joyful, he found a picture of Gianna Maria drinking champagne with a group of friends, giving the camera her middle finger and revealing a fourth finger that was decidedly less diamonded. What a big fucking surprise that the road to true love hadn't been paved with frequent flyer miles.

Rolling his eyes and sighing but armed with ample information to size up Ramirez on first glance, Carlos clicked the *x*'s in the upper right corner of his browser window just as he heard the sound of Alice's voice coming down the hallway.

***

"It feels good to be back," said Shane as he and Alice got off the elevator side by side.

"Is Pris getting any sleep?"

"Surprisingly yes," said Shane. "Theo's not a bad sleeper."

"Any chance you'll be able to start traveling again?" she asked hopefully.

"I'd really prefer not to until my paternity leave is up," said Shane, gently reminding Alice that his coming into the office at all was voluntary and a favor to her. "But I can hold down the fort here. You don't mind doing the travel for a couple more months, do you?"

"Mind? Of course not. I'm grateful you've agreed to come back early." She forced a smile as they rounded the corner.

She *understood*, of course, that Shane wanted to be close to home as he and Priscilla acclimated to having two small children. She knew that despite his cheerful assurances, sleep was probably still erratic and irregular and Pris needed his support.

But it was damned inconvenient that her vice president of sales was off the road for sixteen straight weeks. They were an import-export company, for God's sake, focusing more and more on fine wines from South Africa, South America, New Zealand, and Australia. Deals weren't made in Philadelphia. They were made abroad.

But what could she say? Shane was her brother-in-law,

and he was a top-notch salesman who'd made more inroads with vineyards over the past two years than she'd ever expected. She'd just have to make do, letting his managers take on a little more responsibility and handling big contracts herself. Since she'd hired Shane, her own travels had been cut back appreciably. Trying to look on the bright side, she conceded that she wouldn't necessarily mind hitting the road for a few exotic locales, especially now that Shane could be trusted to run things in her absence.

She paused at Carlos' desk. "Good morning, Carlos."

He grinned at her. "Good morning, Alice."

Ah-leese. Her lips twitched, but she didn't smile.

At SST, only Shane and Carlos called her Alice. Everyone else, without exception, despite age or title, called her Miss Story. But Shane was family, and Carlos? She had a quick flashback to his gray eyes looking up at her as he helped her down from the desk she was standing on.

Carlos was…well, without putting too fine a point on it, *special.* He had believed in her when no one else in the world was willing to give her a chance, and she would never forget that or take it for granted.

"How was your weekend?" she asked.

His tongue slipped out to wet his lips.

You had a date, she thought.

He clenched his jaw once, then cleared his throat.

But it didn't go well.

"Just fine," he answered, nodding once. "And yours?"

She sighed, turning toward her office. "Fine. Busy."

As she sat down at her desk, picking up the iced coffee waiting for her, she looked up to see Carlos standing in the doorway filling the entire space, his body in a crisp white dress shirt and gray suit. He searched her face carefully.

"The luncheon for Priscilla was…a success?"

She shrugged. "She was pleased with the painting. Thanks again for tracking it down for me."

"Of course," he said, still staring at her. Suddenly he nodded, his eyes softening with understanding. "Elizabeth wasn't there."

"Nope. She didn't show."

He winced. "You tried."

"Yes, I did," she said, placing her coffee down on the desk and picking up her granola bar.

"You know better than anyone," he offered gently, "that families can be challenging."

"I do," she agreed, sitting down in her desk chair as she took a bite. Dark-chocolate cherry. Her favorite. "What's on the docket for this morning?"

He stepped into her office and handed her a printout of today's appointments. "Eduardo Ramirez will be here at nine."

"Ramirez," she said, looking up at him, "from…"

"Castillo."

"Oh, right. Of course. Board of directors. But I don't rememb—"

"You didn't. Shane set it up."

"Interesting. Castillo's coming to us?"

Carlos shrugged. "Looks that way."

"Hmm," she hummed, cocking her head to the side. Carlos was good at finding things on the Internet, their seven-year age difference making him more of a digital native than she. "Jump online for me? Find out current deals, stock fluctuations, recent contracts…"

"Wives and girlfriends?" he asked, cocking one eyebrow.

He knows something…

"Not necessary," she said briskly.

...that I don't need to know to drive a business deal.

He made a note in his omnipresent notebook, a two-dollar black-and-white composition book favored by high school teachers everywhere. She'd asked him once why he didn't upgrade to an iPad for note-taking, but he'd just shrugged, told her he preferred his notebooks, and left it at that.

A digital native who prefers paper and pencil.

An old soul.

"Should I ask Shane to stop by?"

She shook her head. "Nope. No need. We'll see what Mr. Ramirez has to say for himself."

Carlos closed the notebook, pressed it against his chest, and then crossed his arms over it. He definitely had something to say, but she watched as he thought better of it, nodding at her once before turning to leave. For a moment she wondered about it, but she was quickly distracted by the sight of her assistant's firm, toned, Justin Trudeau—style butt. Firm and toned, it was hard not to notice, but she'd be mortified if he caught her gawking, even for a second.

She blinked, forcing her eyes up.

"Carlos!" she croaked.

"Yes, Alice?" he asked, pivoting to look at her, his lips twitching.

Ah-leese.

She cleared her throat, positive that her cheeks were pink. He hadn't caught her, but his eyes still twinkled like he knew exactly what she'd been doing.

She raised her chin. "You'll, um, you'll sit in? With Ramirez?"

"Of course," he said, grinning at her before walking back to his desk.

Alice sighed, gnawing off another piece of her granola

bar and rotating her desk chair to look out the window.

Bum-looking notwithstanding, she should have hired someone new to be her assistant when she promoted Carlos to manager. They were two single people under thirty-five, and they'd been working in close quarters for years. Alice had zero designs on Carlos, but he was attractive and she was human. It probably wasn't the smartest arrangement ever, even though there had never been a hint of inappropriateness on either side.

But hiring someone new would mean training them, putting up with their mistakes, and forging a new relationship. She rolled her eyes. Who had time for that? Carlos, with his innate intuition, organizational and research skills, and careful attention to detail, had become indispensable to her. They finished each other's sentences, worked seamlessly together, and enjoyed a shorthand with one another that had been born of necessity and nurtured daily, however inadvertently, over three tumultuous years of building a business together.

And it *was* an appropriate relationship…*aside from the occasional ass-check.* There were no smirks or winks, no cheeky behavior or liberties taken. They didn't share meals together or meet up out of the office unless it was within the context of business. She wouldn't call them friends, per se…though they probably knew one another far better than she knew most of her friends.

She took another bite of her granola bar and frowned.

No. That wasn't true. How could you really know someone without ever seeing their home or celebrating their birthday? Aside from an address in a neighborhood she didn't know, she knew almost nothing about where Carlos lived and what he did after work and with whom. She knew his parents were still in Puerto Rico, but she gathered he had family here. From snippets of phone conversations, she'd figured out that he had a robust dating life, but she had no idea if he had someone special. She didn't know, and she acknowledged it was best that she didn't know. It wasn't any of her business.

But speaking of business, they did work well together; complimenting one another in a way that she'd never seen coming. Her relationship with Carlos was organic, which was probably why she treasured it so much. They were unlikely but intrinsic, like two pieces of wax that had sat side by side under the hot sun until they'd finally melted together.

But *only* here. Only in the office.

She took a deep breath as her thoughts segued from her business relationship with Carlos to her nonexistent personal life.

Wouldn't it be nice, she mused wistfully, *to have that sort of organic comfort in a* romantic *relationship? To be with a man whom I trust implicitly, who looks out for me and has my back and understands me in a way no one else does? Wouldn't it be something if such a man could effortlessly burrow into my heart like he'd been there all along? Wouldn't that be heaven?*

Finishing the last bite of her granola bar and crumpling the wrapper in her palm, she recalled an old F. Scott Fitzgerald quote that had always struck her as particularly on point:

"*They slipped briskly into an intimacy from which they never recovered.*"

She sighed with longing.

That's what Alice wanted, eloquently stated in eleven ordinary words.

She didn't really want her sister to host a gathering for Alice to meet men.

She didn't want to register on Match.com or sign up for

a matchmaking service.

She didn't want to raise her expectations only to have them hopelessly disappointed.

She didn't want the messiness of dating, the wondering if he'd call or not call, the second-guessing of herself, and the chipping away at her own already stingy optimism.

It felt too exhausting even to contemplate because the reality was that Alice didn't want to work at love the way she worked at business.

She turned her chair back around and threw out the crushed wrapper.

All she really wanted was to trip into the arms of the right someone and to never fall out of them again.

Chapter 3

Ramirez was sure laying it on thick.

Carlos bit the side of his cheek, lowering his head to hide a roll of his eyes.

"...but that was back in the eighties," said the older gentleman, who sat—in Carlos' opinion—a little *too* close to Alice on the sofa in her office, taking a little *too* much pleasure in their shared academic connection. "And I *certainly* don't remember Wharton girls being as beautiful as you, Miss Story."

Girls? Carlos snickered inwardly. Alice's father had a bad habit of calling his daughters "gal." Alice *hated* being called a "girl."

Ever the polite businesswoman, however, Alice laughed politely. "You're very kind."

"*No, preciosa!* I'm only being honest!" he insisted, briefly touching her bare arm for emphasis. "I would never have graduated Phi Beta Kappa if there were more girls as pretty as you distracting me from my school work!"

She pulled the sleeves of her cardigan sweater down to her wrists, and this time, her chuckle was slightly less warm, though Carlos doubted that Ramirez noticed since his eyes had dropped to Alice's tits for a long, lusty stare.

Alice cleared her throat, offering her guest a tight smile when he looked up. "I'm intrigued as to the purpose of your visit here today."

Ramirez lost the goofy grin, his face changing to follow the conversation from pleasantries to business matters. "You should know...I'm not here on official Castillo business, Miss Story."

"Oh?"

"No. I'm here with...a proposition."

Everything within Carlos rebelled at Ramirez's use of the word "proposition," and he jerked his head up to look at the older man carefully, searching his face for any hint of disrespect. Finding none, Carlos made a note in his composition book:

A proposition. WTF?

"Is that right?" asked Alice.

Ramirez nodded, clearly enjoying his play on words. "Have you heard of the *Bahía de Plata* vineyards in the Dominican Republic?"

"I haven't."

"I'm not surprised," said Ramirez. "It's not well known. But it *is* doing something quite remarkable. They are the first vineyard of the Caribbean islands making real wine from European grapes...not ginger wine, as they make in Jamaica, or tropical wine from mangoes, but wine made from French Colombard grapes."

"Fascinating," said Alice, leaning forward a touch, her brown eyes rapt with attention.

He grinned at her, almost preening as she took the bait. "I've tasted it...it's very good."

Alice nodded. "Tell me more about it."

"Of course," he said, a fisherman with a big one on his

hook. "But do you think I could have a cup of coffee first?"

"Coffee? Oh. Of course. We should have already offered you a refreshment." She turned to Carlos, who sat in an office chair across the coffee table from them. "Carlos, would you mind?"

Generally, he wouldn't mind at all. He'd fetched coffee a million times or more for Alice and her guests, but the smirk on Ramirez's face made Carlos bristle. He sensed that the older man was laughing at him, a thought confirmed by his next words.

"How *refreshing* that gender roles are reversed here, Miss Story."

"Reversed?"

He gestured between Carlos and Alice. "A man getting the coffee…a woman in charge."

Carlos placed his notebook on the table, lifting his eyes to Alice's, which flashed once in pique. "I wouldn't say the roles are *reversed*, señor. Everyone has a fair chance to prove themselves here, and Carlos is one of my best employees."

"What a woman!" Ramirez chuckled, shifting his glance back to Carlos. "I like it black and strong, *por favor.*"

"*Un placer,*" said Carlos without smiling. He looked at his boss, softening his expression for her. "Alice?"

"I'll take a water, please," she said, then turned back to Ramirez. "Please tell me more about Caribbean wine-making."

Carlos stepped to the door, leaving it wide open as he headed down the corridor and around the corner to the pantry, seething a bit inside.

In *Puerto Rican* culture, which Carlos shared with Ramirez, *machismo* was still alive and well. And though it was a changing concept, with more and more women taking leadership positions in business and politics, the idea of a man being subservient to a woman in the workplace was still cause for amusement among some, especially someone like Ramirez, who was twenty-five years older than Carlos and far more successful.

Traditional machismo had dictated that men were breadwinners and rule makers, while women tended the home and children. However, with dual-income households more the norm these days, Carlos was used to seeing his friends help with dishes after dinner or take care of the children while their wives or girlfriends were at work. Times were definitely changing.

That said, in Carlos' generation, the sort of *machismo* that still mattered greatly was the kind in which one man didn't allow another man to step to what was his. In a bar or club, for instance, if Carlos was dancing with his woman and another man stepped up to dance with her, he'd take care of it quickly. How? For starters, he'd tell the other man in no uncertain terms that his advances were unwelcome. Should the interloper be persistent, Carlos would have no problem decking him. (And frankly, if he didn't, his woman and peers would wonder where his balls were hiding.)

Why would he get physical? For two reasons: One, because the unwelcome attention would be offensive to Carlos' date and he wouldn't allow such disrespect to go unchecked. And two, because Puerto Rican men felt, under no uncertain terms, that there was honor in caring for what was theirs.

He grabbed a bottle of cold water from the fridge and poured Ramirez a cup of coffee, stopping short of spitting in it as he reminded himself, *Alice isn't yours.*

She was his boss, but she didn't belong to him. He needed to tamp down his natural instinct to tell Ramirez to quit looking at her breasts and stop touching her arm. She wasn't his to protect.

***

"In *Bahía de Plata*, they get only thirty-six inches of rain per year, which, as you may know, is optimum for cultivating grapes and far below the average for a Caribbean island," said Ramirez. "And I have tasted the wines, Miss Story. They are…well, I believe they are on par with French wines."

"Really?"

Carlos reentered the office, placing the beverages on the coffee table and resuming his seat.

"Oh, yes. With the support of winemakers from Portugal and Spain, the vineyard currently produces two annual harvests. And there is a resort, as well…with beautiful villas, a hotel, clubhouse, restaurant, marina, shops, spa, an airstrip…"

"Agritourism at its best," said Alice. She glanced up at Carlos. "Are you getting all this?"

"Every word."

"It is…such a beautiful spot, and the local people are hired to help cultivate and harvest the grapes, so it's brought jobs to the region as well."

"My goodness," murmured Alice, wondering why she hadn't heard about *Bahía de Plata* sooner.

It wasn't often, in this day and age, that someone, somewhere, tried an ancient method to create something new and was met with such success. If the Dominican Republic was making European-quality wines, the possibilities for importation were endless!

She thought of all the restaurants in Philadelphia that served Caribbean food and came up with twenty off the top of her head. Add New York, Washington, and Boston to the equation and there must be hundreds. Right now, most of those restaurants served South American or Spanish wines so that they at least *sounded* right on the wine list. But her mind whirled at the thought of offering these businesses wines that were actually from the Caribbean.

"Are you an investor, Mr. Ramirez?"

He chuckled, shaking his head. "Sadly, no. I didn't hear about the project until 2014, and by then *Bahía de Plata* was ably assisted by others. But I have been keeping a close eye on it."

"Are they interested in exporting?"

"I couldn't say," he answered affably.

Alice frowned. "Forgive me, but you do know that Story Sisters Trading is a beverage import-export company?"

"Of course," he said with a grin. "But you are also Alice Story, the heiress."

Alice leaned away as Carlos jerked his head up from his note-taking, gray eyes narrowing at their guest.

"Mr. Ramirez, I don't see how my personal finances—"

"Your sister, Margaret Story Winslow…she owns a local vineyard, yes?"

"Yes. The Five Sisters."

"Are you an investor?"

Alice nodded. "Not a major one, but yes, my sister Priscilla and I both have a small stake in the Five Sisters."

"So it's safe to say that you're a wine-making family? You and your sisters?"

"Not really," she said. "I invested in Margaret's vineyard years ago when she was first getting started. Priscilla invested after she got married. But neither Priscilla nor I have anything to do with Margaret's operation."

"Better still," said Ramirez, winking at her.

Because he was older than she, she let this slight pass, just as she had with his use of the word "girl" to describe her. But her patience was definitely wearing thin. She looked up at Carlos, whose eyes were cool. He obviously shared her reserved sentiments about the very charming, game-playing Ramirez.

"With respect, señor, I think it would save us both a bit of time if you told me exactly why you're here."

"Cutting to the chase," he said, nodding at her with a sly smile. "I respect that, Miss. Story. I *heard* you were all business. But I confess, señorita, I didn't believe a woman so young and beautiful could be so focused. You have proved me wrong."

With a serene smile, Alice stared back at him, unwilling to engage in any more of his flattery and waiting for him to continue with the reason for his visit. If he didn't, she would ask Carlos to please escort him out, and by the look on her assistant's face, she felt certain he'd relish the task.

Ramirez's playful grin faded, and he reached for his coffee, taking a sip before replacing the cup to the saucer. He looked up at Carlos. "You do wonderful work in the kitchen."

Taking his cue from Alice, Carlos stared back at their guest, unflinching, waiting for him to answer his boss's question.

"Ay! You two are no fun!" cried Ramirez, chuckling to himself. "Business it is!"

Finally.

"I am from the island of Puerto Rico. Do you know it?" he asked Alice.

"I've never been."

"Well, it is a wonderful place, I assure you. And recently I have made a particular discovery. In the southern part of the island, near my home in Ponce, there is a valley that receives about thirty-six inches of rain per year. It has almost identical conditions to the area of *Bahía de Plata*."

Alice nodded. "I see."

"Do you? Well, let me illuminate you further…I have bought the land. All of it. Four hundred acres. And I intend to start my own vineyard there, following the model established in *Bahía de Plata*."

In her role as company owner, Alice made many deals, but there were only a few that had made her heart start to race like this one. To be in on the ground floor of such an operation? To be an investor? Why, she would have input on production, sales, and marketing. She could have exclusive import-export rights. She could—

"I see your mind whirling, Miss Story," said Ramirez, reaching out to place his hand on her knee.

Carlos cleared his throat loudly, and Ramirez looked up at the younger man, smirking at him before removing his hand with a sigh.

"You're seeking investors?" asked Carlos, his voice clipped.

"No," he said. "Partners."

"Me?" asked Alice.

"You and your sisters. We require six million dollars to get the operation started."

"What are you contributing, señor?" asked Carlos evenly.

"The other six million," he answered lightly. Turning to Alice, he cocked his head to the side and smiled at her. "I have confidence in this project."

"It *is* intriguing," said Alice. "But I'd need more information, of course. And I would have to speak to my sisters."

"I would like to invite you, Miss Story, to visit my home in Ponce," said Ramirez. "I can show you the land I've purchased and the plans our landscape architect from *Bahía de Plata* has drawn up. You will fall in love there," he said, his voice low and almost seductive. "I promise."

Alice stared into his bright-blue eyes, feeling slightly hypnotized by his promise and presence and the marvelous opportunity he'd brought to her doorstep. She loved the idea of partial ownership of a vineyard in the Caribbean, especially if her sisters were her partners too.

Alice turned to Carlos. "I'd need to see *Bahía de Plata* first, of course. Look into it?"

Carlos nodded.

"I could…meet you there?" suggested Ramirez.

"No, thank you," said Alice quickly, uncertain of how she felt about the charming, overconfident older man and his innuendo. "But I will come to Ponce after I've seen *Bahía de Plata*…if I think the project has merit and promise."

Ramirez was handsome. She couldn't deny that. He was also well educated and successful. And his inappropriate touches and suggestive double entendre could be cultural— Latino men were, after all, notorious flirts.

But all the same, he would need to be managed if they engaged in any sort of business deal together. Alice didn't date people she worked with. Not ever. And that would include Ramirez, should she decide to invest in his Ponce vineyard. If he persisted in his flattery, she would need to make her unavailability clear at some point, though she hoped it wouldn't come to that. It would bruise his ego and could negatively affect their efficacy in working together.

"I greatly look forward to seeing the *Bahía de Plata* operation."

"And I will be on my knees night and day, hoping you believe it has…promise."

He took her hand, drawing it to his lips and kissing it before returning it to her lap and standing.

So surprised by his gesture, she hadn't been able to pull her hand away in time, but Alice felt the kiss all over her body—the soft, gentle touch of lips to skin. It had been a long time since she'd been kissed—anywhere—and her heart fluttered from the contact.

"Thank you, señor," she said, her voice slightly breathless, certain she was blushing but determined to end their meeting as professionally as possible, "for bringing this idea to me. Please e-mail any information to Carlos. I will be in touch soon."

"I will count the minutes," he said, holding out his hand. "Adios, Miss Story."

Alice shook it, careful to drop it quickly.

"Adios, señor."

***

Carlos seethed inside as he showed Ramirez to the door.

Not only was he an asshole to Carlos with all that coffee bullshit, but he'd been totally inappropriate with Alice. Gaping at her tits? Touching her knee? Kissing her hand? He was taking liberties, and they both knew it.

"*Dime,*" said Ramirez from behind as Carlos led him toward the reception area, "*de donde eres?*" *Where are you from?*

"*Puerto Rico,*" he said without turning around.

"*De verdad? De que parte?*" *Really? What part?*

"*Toa Baja.*"

"*¡Y yo de Guaynabo! ¡Tremenda coincidencia!*" *What a coincidence!*

"*Supongo que sí,*" he answered without much enthusiasm. *I suppose.*

Carlos opened the glass door to the reception area, holding it for Ramirez. Once they were both in the lobby, he let it swing back gently.

"You don't like me," said Ramirez, smirking at Carlos.

"I don't know you," said Carlos, though he was lying. He knew guys like Ramirez. Rich, entitled assholes from little islands. Little kings in their own big heads.

"You think you do."

Carlos ignored this and nodded at Susan in greeting as they walked past the reception desk. He opened the glass doors and led Ramirez to the elevator lobby.

But Ramirez wasn't finished testing him yet.

"*Tu jefa…está que estilla.*" *Your boss…she's hot.*

Carlos flinched, clenching his jaw as he turned to face Ramirez.

Sizing up the older man quickly, Carlos knew that, physically at least, he could have Ramirez on his back, begging for mercy, in two seconds flat. Ramirez was only athletic in a country club sort of way, without any real muscle tone. And his face—which had probably lured a thousand women to his bed at one time, had a fair amount of creases and sun spots up close. It wasn't quite as handsome as it likely had been twenty years ago when he was in his prime. Still, between the two of them, Ramirez was in the position of power: older, wealthier, established, and a possible future partner to Carlos' boss. Throwing a punch in the defense of a woman who didn't belong to him would be stupid, and no matter how much loyalty Alice had to Carlos, she would have no option but to fire him.

He answered in English, his voice gritty with anger. "I'll ask you to use a more respectful tone when speaking to me about Miss Story, *me entiendes?*"

"Ha! Because I should be concerned for your fragile sensibilities?" scoffed Ramirez.

"Because," said Carlos, cracking his knuckles, "I'll deck you if you ever insult her in front of me again."

"Was that a threat?" asked Ramirez, stepping to Carlos,

puffing up his smaller, less muscular chest until it grazed Carlos' suit jacket.

"A warning," said Carlos, stepping back as the elevator door opened and gesturing with his hand for Ramirez to enter.

"With all that fetching coffee and taking notes, I was *wondering* where your balls were," said Ramirez, chuckling as he entered the elevator and turned to face Carlos. "Good to see you still have them...*muchacho.*"

It was on the tip of Carlos' tongue to tell Ramirez to go to hell, but the doors closed before he could say another word. He stood in the lobby for a moment gathering his wits. He let out a long breath and unclenched his fists.

He didn't appreciate feeling emasculated—what man did?—but *cabrónes* like Ramirez were a dime a dozen, and they didn't really understand the most recent generation of Boricua men. Men who had to adapt to a changing world and leave traditional gender roles behind if they wanted to succeed in their personal and professional lives.

Sighing as he turned and stalked back into the office, he swung into the pantry and pulled a Coke from the fridge, uncapping it and taking a cold, burning sip as he returned to Alice. She was focused, with hawklike intensity, on her computer screen, not looking up as he walked in.

"What do you think?" she asked.

"Solid opportunity."

"About Ramirez."

"You know what I think," he said without skipping a beat.

"He can be managed," she said, but her voice held a hint of uncertainty.

Ramirez had been pretty bold. "I don't know."

She bit her lip, typing something else into the

computer. "Do you know this area? Ponce?"

He nodded, sitting in one of the two guest chairs in front of her desk. "Sure. Every college kid in Puerto Rico has partied in Ponce at some point. It's on the southern coast of the island."

She turned to him. "And you're from…"

"The north."

"But you've been there? To Ponce?"

"Many times."

She took a deep breath and sighed. "Okay, good. Find out about land, about him, about the rainfall. Look into *Bahía de Plata* and find out if we can visit as business interests, not tourists. I want to see how they run things."

"You want a tour of the property? As an importer?"

Alice thought for a moment. "Yes. But make it clear I'm only seeking one-year contracts. We'll make it worth their while to welcome us, but I don't want them to have expectations beyond a year. If I go into business with Ramirez, I'll sell Ponce wines once they're available."

"Got it," he said. "Anything else?"

She nodded. "Book two tickets to the Dominican Republic. I want to stay in *Bahía de Plata* for a day or two and check out their operation."

"Right. And then on to Ponce?"

She grimaced, then nodded. "Yes. As long as I'm down there, I'll go check out the land Ramirez has acquired and compare it to what I see in *Bahía de Plata*."

Carlos stood from his chair, pushed it under the lip of her desk, and scribbled something on his notepad. "The tickets…for you and…?"

She cleared her throat, her cheeks flushing just a touch as she raised her chin. "Shane isn't traveling again until October."

"Then…?" he asked, his heart fluttering and thumping for no good reason.

"You. You'll accompany me instead."

His breath caught. He knew it was coming, but he still hadn't expected it. And he certainly didn't know what to do with the riot of emotions he was having at the prospect of traveling with Alice for a week.

"Me," he whispered.

The color in her cheeks deepened.

"Yes. Shane said you did quite well in Chile."

"Uh…okay, then. Thank you for your confidence in me, Alice."

"Ah-leese," she murmured softly, then gulped, nodding curtly and returning her attention to her computer screen. "You know…if all goes well, you should consider putting in for a promotion to the sales team. I'd hate to lose you, but I'd never hold you back."

Her words set off a dual reaction inside of him—gratitude and sorrow colliding. Being promoted to a sales associate would be a huge step toward a brighter future, but not working directly for Alice anymore? He winced inside, the thought pinching his heart, making him wonder which was more important to him.

"When did you want to go?"

"My schedule's open." She remained focused on her computer. "The sooner the better, if that works for you."

"The sooner it is," he said, turning away from her and the unexpectedly confusing feelings that this morning's events had uncovered.

Chapter 4

"Caribbean vineyard owners. I love it," said Margaret, crossing her legs and taking a sip of seltzer water as she sat down on the couch beside Alice. "I'm in."

"I haven't even outlined the proposal yet," Alice scoffed, staring at Margaret as she accepted a cup of cappuccino from Priscilla.

"I don't care. I love it too," said Priscilla, sitting down in a chair across from Margaret as she cradled a sleeping Theo in her arms. "If Meggie's in, I'm in."

"You're both crazy," said Alice. "All I said was that I might know of a vineyard in the Caribbean that needs investors."

"I know you well enough to know you wouldn't even mention it to us unless you thought it was a good deal," said Priscilla. "Besides, Shane filled me in."

"Yes. Not to mention, unlike you," said Margaret, "I have been following the developments in *Bahía de Plata* for two years now and kicking myself that I wasn't in on the ground floor."

Alice had e-mailed her sisters on Monday afternoon about the Ponce vineyard deal, and Priscilla had invited both of them to her house for dinner and to discuss it further the following evening. However, because bedtime was especially chaotic with a toddler and newborn, Alice and Shane had ended up grilling steaks outside while Margaret made a salad inside and Priscilla bathed the kids. Now Shane was putting Kaitlyn to bed so the sisters had a little time to talk.

He'd already weighed in yesterday, telling Alice that he definitely thought it was worth her while to check out *Bahía de Plata* and encouraging her to take Carlos with her. When she said that she'd already invited Carlos to accompany her, Shane had nodded, telling her that it was "about time."

More evidence that Carlos was due for a promotion to Shane's sales team.

Hmm.

She sighed inwardly. She would never hold Carlos back, of course…but what would she do without him? Perhaps she could insist that he train his replacement before moving internally. This thought, however, which should have reassured her, didn't. She hated the idea of training and working with someone new.

No. That wasn't the whole truth.

What she *really* hated was the idea of losing Carlos by her side.

"Alice?" prompted Priscilla. "Alice!"

"What? Yes!" She shot a glance to Margaret. "Kicking yourself. Right."

"Someone seems a little distracted tonight," said Priscilla, a slight singsong quality to her voice. "Are you all right?"

"What do you mean?"

"I mean…Margaret just went on and on about the sustainability of the *Bahía de Plata* vineyards, and you were zoned out like you'd just been hypnotized."

"Don't be ridiculous." She turned to Margaret. "I heard every word."

Margaret chuckled softly. "So what's my major fear about the success of Ponce?"

Alice cleared her throat. "I…well, that is, um…"

Margaret took mercy on her older sister. "Puerto Ricans are urban people. Only six percent are farmers, and most of the farms are in the interior part of the island, not on the coast. Are you sure we'll have the necessary manpower for a project this big? How will you get enough farming staff to relocate?"

"A good question for me to ask Ramirez once I'm there."

There…with Carlos.

In the moments before she'd told Carlos that he would be accompanying her to the Caribbean on business, she hadn't felt any specific emotion. But in the split seconds that followed, she'd been nearly overwhelmed by how much she suddenly *felt* at the prospect of traveling alone with him. Feelings that she'd never expected: excitement, anticipation, and a foreign, almost giddy elation had flushed her cheeks, surprising and embarrassing her.

And he'd—well, frankly, he'd seemed off-balance too, blinking at her in surprise as he whispered, "Me."

Margaret cleared her throat meaningfully, and Alice looked up to see her sisters exchange conspiratorial grins.

"Speaking of *Ramirez*…we'd *love* to know a little bit more about him," said Priscilla with a shit-eating grin.

"I looked him up," said Margaret, her lips tilting up in a small smile. "He's successful, handsome…"

"And eligible!" Priscilla said. "His house in Ponce? O-M-G, Allie. It looked like a palace on Zillow."

Alice shot her little sister a glare. It had been years since any of them had called her "Allie," a family nickname she had insisted they stop when she started high school, preferring the more formal and proper "Alice." "What's Zillow?"

"A realtor website," said Margaret. "It's called *Hacienda del Mar.*"

"The website? I thought it was called Zillow."

"It is," said Priscilla, her smile dreamy. "Can you imagine the views?"

"Twelve thousand square feet of space," said Margaret wistfully, "on a hill overlooking the Caribbean."

Alice had caught up enough by now to understand that her sisters had been checking out Ramirez online via a website called Zillow that apparently showcased his palatial house.

"Ahhhhh," sighed the younger Story sisters in unison, batting their eyes at Alice.

Alice rolled hers.

"Subtlety, thy name is neither Margaret nor Priscilla."

"There is nothing wrong with a May–December romance!" trilled Priscilla.

"May–*December*?" repeated Alice. "He's hardly at death's door, Pris!"

"Of course he's not! More like…*September*!" said Margaret, frowning briefly at Priscilla before brightening her smile for Alice. "He looks very…er, *virile* to me."

"*Very*," said Priscilla, nodding in agreement. "And if he can't get it up, there's always Viagra."

"Pris!" reprimanded Margaret. "Not helpful!"

"Viagra!" exclaimed Alice, her head ping-ponging back and forth between her sisters, her cheeks flushing with heat as her mind created an unwanted snapshot of Ramirez naked. "No! Stop!"

"He went to Wharton," sang Priscilla. "Admit it: huge coincidence!"

"*Not* a coincidence," insisted Alice. "Plenty of people go to Wharton."

"Okay…but he *is* well educated," said Margaret, leaning closer.

"Yes…"

"Which is important," said Priscilla, beaming down at her sleeping baby. "You know, for father material."

Whoa. What? *Father* material?

Priscilla held up four fingers, lowering them one by one. "Hot…established…rich…and well educated. We think you should go for him!"

"Oh, is that what you think?" she asked, sarcasm heavy in her voice. She set her coffee cup on the table and looked at Margaret accusatorily, her "Pris-is-one-thing-but-you-should-know-better" look.

Margaret looked appropriately sheepish. "Well…he *has* sort of dropped into your lap."

"No. He's offered me a business deal. Full stop."

"A fortuitous meeting!" declared Priscilla.

"He's twenty years older than me," Alice informed them.

"So what?" said Priscilla with a bright smile. "He's a silver fox!"

"You're ridiculous," said Alice. "I don't even know him."

"Did he seem to *like* you?" asked Margaret gently.

Alice sighed.

Yes. Yes, he did seem to like me, she thought, remembering the way he'd touched and flattered her. And certainly the attention hadn't been entirely in her own head since Carlos had looked murderous by the end of the meeting.

Wait a second.

Why *did he look murderous?*

Why did Ramirez bother him so much?

Could it have anything to do with…me?

Her heart leapt and fluttered for a second as she considered this question…before taking a deep breath and answering it logically for herself.

Of course it had nothing to do with her.

Carlos' aversion to the older businessman was the result of Ramirez's pointed barbs about fetching the coffee and taking notes. Ramirez had emasculated Carlos with his comments. Carlos had a right to dislike him.

And yet…niggled the annoying little seed of doubt that had already been planted in her mind.

When Ramirez had called Alice an "heiress," Carlos had bristled, his eyes narrowing in distaste. And when Ramirez had touched Alice's leg, Carlos had leaned forward in his chair and cleared his throat loudly. She had glanced up to find his body coiled and tense, like an angry lion ready to pounce.

Was it just loyalty? A sense of protectiveness toward his boss?

Or…*something more?*

Her body tingled as she recalled the way Carlos' breath had hitched when she told him he'd be accompanying her to Puerto Rico. She'd heard it catch, and it had made the flush in her cheeks deepen. She'd felt so *aware* of him in that moment, suddenly realizing that, coworkers or not, they'd be spending a week together in the Caribbean.

Alone.

"Look at that dreamy smile, Meggie!"

Alice blinked, looking up at Priscilla. "What smile?"

"You *like* him!"

Her eyes widened as she heard rapid-fire words in her head: *No! No, I don't. He's my assistant. My employee. That would be wrong. I absolutely refuse to have any feelings for him beyond—*

"His first name is Eduardo, right?" asked Margaret, and Alice turned to her, realizing that her sisters were still talking about Ramirez.

"Yes! Eduardo," Alice replied. "Eduardo Ramirez. That's who we're talking about. Mm-hm. That is his name."

Margaret stared at her older sister, cocking her head to the side and nodding like she was trying to figure something out.

"Ooooh!" squealed Priscilla. "You're so flustered! I love it!"

"I'm *not* flustered," protested Alice, drinking the rest of her coffee before rising from the couch and taking her empty cup into the kitchen.

At least not about Eduardo Ramirez.

***

Alice was acting strange.

Real strange.

And with a car picking them up at their respective apartments tomorrow morning at six o'clock and six fifteen, Carlos wondered whether or not he should say something. Otherwise, they risked spending the whole week in uncomfortable silence.

Had Monday been a little awkward after she told him he'd be going to the Dominican Republic and Puerto Rico with her? Yes. A little. Hearing her say that he'd be accompanying her...*to the Caribbean...for a week...alone...*had set off a totally unexpected chain reaction inside his body. His blood, which was already running hot in response to Ramirez's affronts and liberties, had heated up to volcanic levels for totally different reasons, his stupid heart stuttering at the thought of finally being alone with Alice out of the office. But his sweet, steamy high had plummeted when she told him he should consider transferring to Shane's group. In theory, he knew it was not a rejection but a vote of confidence. Still, the suggestion stung, and he'd left her office feeling cold.

As for Alice? She'd hunkered down behind closed doors for the remainder of the day, working quietly at her desk. On a normal day, she called him into her office no fewer than a dozen times, asking for updates or numbers, so Monday had been noticeably quiet. When he'd knocked on her door at the end of the day to present the information he'd gathered about *Bahía de Plata*, she'd asked him to leave it on her desk instead of stopping what she was doing to go over it together. He'd stared at her bent head, realizing she was purposely keeping her eyes averted. When she didn't look up after several awkward seconds, he placed the file folder on her desk and bid her good night.

Since then, even though he sat ten feet from her office door, their contact had been mostly limited to e-mails.

On Tuesday, he had e-mailed her the itinerary for their trip: outbound flight for two from Philadelphia International to Santo Domingo on Thursday morning, with a two-hour stop in Atlanta, a transfer to *Bahía de Plata*, and three nights at the *Gran Palacio de Plata*, the Silver Palace Resort Hotel. On Sunday, when most Caribbean businesses were closed for the day, they would fly via chartered plane from Santo Domingo to Ponce, where Ramirez planned to collect them from the airport at three o'clock. When speaking to Ramirez's assistant, Carlos had asked for a hotel recommendation nearby at which to make reservations for himself and Alice. He was informed, however, that Ramirez insisted on hosting Miss Story at his pretentiously named home, *Hacienda del Mar.* She had suggested to book a room at a local hotel, the Howard Johnson's Ponce, for Carlos.

"*Está solo una milla de Hacienda del Mar,*" she explained.

One mile too far, Carlos had thought, thanking the assistant for her advice but ultimately ignoring it.

Fuck the Howard Johnson's.

Carlos didn't trust Ramirez with Alice as far as he could throw him. Furthermore, he dared Ramirez to look into his eyes, once he arrived *with* Alice, and tell Carlos in front of her he didn't have room for him to stay at his mansion. Ramirez wouldn't have the *cojones* to be so rude in person, nor would he jeopardize Alice's good opinion by refusing hospitality to her employee. Which meant that Ramirez was stuck with him, and Alice—*whether she wanted it or not*—would have Carlos' protection.

Not, likely being the case, if lack of eye contact and communication was any indication.

Which brought him full circle: Alice was acting really strange, and Carlos decided to talk to her on Wednesday morning.

Instead of placing her coffee and granola bar on her desk per usual, he kept them at his desk, eager to have an excuse to step into her office when she arrived and hoping to smooth things out between them. It was going to be an awfully awkward week if she couldn't even look him in the eyes.

Sure enough, at 8:01, Alice sailed by his desk en route to her office and murmured, "Good morning." After she'd had a moment to get settled, he entered her office uninvited, closing the door behind him.

She looked up in surprise, her eyes wide, her cheeks flushing instantly.

"Good morning," he said, approaching her desk and

placing her coffee and breakfast bar on her blotter.

"Good morning," she murmured, pulling the coffee to her lips and taking a sip.

"Alice," he asked, placing his hands on his hips, "is everything...okay?"

Her face jerked up, her brown eyes meeting his gray. "Why do you ask?"

He sighed, pulling out a guest chair and taking a seat. "We've been working together for three years now."

She nodded, gulping softly. "Yes."

He searched her eyes, but she gave away nothing.

"I can tell when you're upset about something," he said, smoothing his tie with a slide of his palm before looking up at her. "And you seem...well, I'm just gonna be honest: it feels like you're avoiding me."

"I'm not," she said, her shoulders relaxing as she puffed out a held breath. "Can I be honest too?"

"Please," he said, bracing himself internally.

"I thought you were coming in here to ask for a transfer to Shane's group."

This surprised him. Frankly, he'd barely considered the possible promotion or how it could fit in with attending grad school since she'd mentioned it on Monday, and he certainly hadn't decided about whether or not he was ready to make a change. But, huh—apparently *she'd* been thinking about it quite a bit.

"No," he said. "To be honest, Alice, I haven't thought about it much."

"Why not?"

He shrugged. "I've been busy, I guess...doing the job I have."

"Well, you *should* think about it," she said.

In fact, she said this with such conviction that it made

him wonder about her motives. Did she want to get rid of him? Did she want a new assistant and moving him to Shane's group was a means to that end?

"Is that what *you* want? For me to work for Shane?" he asked, holding his breath as he waited for her to answer.

"I…" She dropped his eyes, looking down at her desk. She slipped her bottom lip between her teeth, a gesture he *rarely* saw from confident, assertive Alice. The last time he'd seen her look like this was after a fight she'd had with her sister Elizabeth. It was a tell. An *emotional* tell. Finally, she answered him softly: "No."

He leaned forward, his foolish heart taking flight and willing her to look at him. "Then…?"

"But you *should*. You *should* be promoted." Raising her head, her eyes were sorry, her lips turned down like she was disappointed in herself. "If you stay here, working for me, it means I'm holding you back."

"Only if you're *keeping* me from moving." He tented his hands. "Alice, I like my job. I'm—well, I think I'm good at it."

"You *are*," she said quickly. "*Very* good. But Shane says you're wonderful in the field." She took a deep breath and sighed. "In your present position—as office manager and executive assistant—there's nowhere left to go. I can't promote you any higher or increase your salary any further. But in sales? The sky's the limit."

His eyes traced her face—landing on her temple and staring at the way she pulled her blonde hair back so tightly from her crown into a bun every day. Did it hurt, he wondered, as he had many times before, to wear her hair like that? Did it ache a little all day, every day?

"Is this why you've been avoiding me?"

She reached for her coffee, shrugging delicately. "It

would be wrong to keep you on as my assistant if you're capable of more."

"I like being your assistant," he said gently. "Besides, that's not all I do. I'm the office manager too. And when I'm needed, I pitch in on the sales team—"

"No," said Alice, shaking her head. "Wearing too many hats means you'll be wearing none well. Besides, you didn't leave the mail room to be my assistant forever."

Maybe I did, he thought, raising his chin as he looked into her eyes. "You assume I have as much business ambition as you."

She looked back at him, and her eyebrows creased, as though she was learning something important about him for the first time, and he realized that she was. Of course he hadn't wanted to work in a mail room for the rest of his life...but right hand to a CEO? Office manager of a twenty-five-person office? Occasional sales team translator? Why couldn't these three pieces be incorporated into one position custom made for him? Why did he have to choose between them?

"You're right. I *do* assume that. Am I wrong?" She propped her elbow on the desk and rested her chin in her palm, her eyes troubled. "I've never asked as long as we've been working together. What are your ambitions, Carlos? What do you want?"

He thought for a moment, no easy answer arriving at the forefront of his mind. In terms of having a home, wife, and children, yes—he had a certain timeline in mind for when he wanted those things and was just starting to feel a steadily growing internal pressure to settle down. But that wasn't what Alice was talking about—she was discussing business. And where business was concerned? He had a completed application for grad school in his desk that he still hadn't sent. His ambition was less focused, his goals less rigid than hers.

"I'm not totally sure." He smiled at her. "Is that an easy question for you to answer?"

"Of course. I have…five-, ten-, twenty-, and thirty-year plans for my professional life."

"*You do?*" he blurted out, his eyes wide.

"Absolutely. It's the framework for my whole future."

"Whew," he breathed, rubbing the stubble on his chin with his thumb and forefinger. "That's a lot of planning."

"How else would I know where I'm going?"

"I don't know." He shrugged. "You could…see what life offers? Make your decisions as they come?"

"I don't *wait* for change," she said. "I make it *happen*." She took a deep breath and sighed, assuming he didn't understand what she was saying and further clarifying her thoughts by adding, "I wanted to start my own company. I wanted to be the CEO and president of that company. Lead it. Manage its direction. Build it."

"You're fulfilling your goals," he said with admiration. "You're meeting them."

"Yes, I am." She took another sip of her coffee and unwrapped her KIND bar. "So you don't have *any* professional goals mapped out?"

"I…well, I was working in a mail room when I was offered something better. And now…"

"You're being offered *another* something better," she said.

Would it be better? he wondered.

Junior members of the sales team were expected to travel for two to three weeks at a time, visiting vineyards in Chile, Argentina, New Zealand, Australia, or South Africa. Instead of being around for weekend family gatherings or downtime at home, he'd be on the road. A lot.

"My professional goals are"—he cleared his throat, rubbing his hands together—"undefined, I guess, but definitely more modest than yours. I didn't grow up in a mansion in Haverford, Alice. I'm already earning more than the rest of my siblings by a significant amount." He cocked his head to the side, knowing he was about to share more with her about his family than he ever had before. "My mother and father run a small restaurant—*Casa Vega*—in my hometown of Toa Baja."

"*Casa Vega*. Vega, like your last name."

"*Sí*," he said, grinning at her as he pictured the tiny café with bright walls and diner-style tables that sat four each. *What would Philadelphia heiress Alice Story think of it*, he wondered. "Just a popular little place serving good rice and beans. *Mofongos*—"

"What is that?" she asked, taking another bite of her breakfast bar.

"*Mofongos*?" he asked, his eyes widening at her question. *It's only the national dish of Puerto Rico!* "It's mashed green plantains served with fresh seafood or meat."

"Plantains?" she asked, sipping her coffee as she looked at him over the rim of her cup. "I've never had that. It's like bananas, right?"

Not the way Mama makes them.

"Ahhh-leeese," he said, laying on his accent and drawing out her name. Her eyes grew wider, and he chuckled again. "We're gonna to have to find some good *mofongos* for you to try while we're there. You're gonna love it."

"Did you work there? At the restaurant?"

"Yes. Of course. We all did. Me and my brothers and sisters. Some of my cousins too."

"A family business."

"Exactly," he said.

"Would you have inherited it? If you'd stayed?"

He nodded. "Definitely. Co-ownership with my siblings or cousins. But you must understand, I would've been a busboy or waiter for years until then. And...well, I didn't want that, even if it led to me owning *Casa Vega* one day. I wanted more than that."

As a rule, Alice didn't smile very much—it wasn't part of her comfortable resting face, but she had been smiling, just slightly, as he spoke about *Casa Vega*. Now her lips faded into a line, then turned down slightly as she dropped her eyes to her desk.

"More," she said softly. "Like a career in business."

"Business classes came easily to me at university. Seemed as good a path as any," he said, trying to follow her sudden shift in mood.

"Remember the way my father ran his business?"

"Of course."

"He was..." She set down her granola bar, staring at it for a moment. "He was a terrible boss. Unfair. Prejudiced. Holding back employees that—"

Carlos narrowed his eyes. "You are nothing like him, Alice."

Her eyes blazed suddenly as though lit by a fire from deep within her. "I will fight against...being like him...with all the strength I have."

Carlos stared at her, moved by the gritty passion in her voice, realizing that she was sharing a core truth of her adult person, knowing that she had started Alice Story Imports, in part, to prove that she could be a better employer, a better *person* than her father. Here and now, with thirteen words, she was showing him who she was, and Carlos finally understood the truth behind her recent avoidance of him on every level.

If she didn't promote a hardworking employee—if he stayed on as her assistant and didn't accept a promotion to Shane's team—she would blame herself for doing to him what her father had done to her. In Alice's mind, she would be denying Carlos a better future in the same way her father had denied her any meaningful advancement at Story Imports.

She took a deep breath, threw out her half-eaten granola bar, and raised her chin. "When we return from Puerto Rico, you'll be promoted to Shane's group and given a commensurate raise. It's for the best."

"Wait. What?"

"It's done."

"Alice, I don't even…"

He was about to say, *I don't even know if that's what I want.*

But he stopped himself because that would be crazy, right? It would be crazy to close the door on a possible promotion and a raise.

So why did he feel such apprehension? Such reluctance to shake her hand and accept the change with enthusiasm?

"I refuse to hold you back," she said definitively, turning away from him and back to her monitor. "I'll let Shane know to get the wheels in motion ASAP. It'll happen two weeks after we return from Ponce. I'll expect you to train your replacement the day after we return."

"Of course," he murmured, stunned that everything was happening so fast when his gut reaction was to ask her for more time to think it over. "Alice, I'd actually like to—"

"You'll still be here," she said, her voice uncharacteristically emotional, and somehow it felt like she was speaking more to herself than to him. "And that's good because you're…well, you're *important*, Carlos." She cleared her throat. "Important to this company."

He stared at her, uncertain of what he wanted to say, needing more time to process everything that had just happened but feeling like the sand as the tide came in, about to disappear under the relentless forward motion of the approaching waves.

"Congratulations," she said with a back-to-business nod. "Now, can you hold my calls this morning? Also, I'd like to see the exportation numbers on the *Bahía de Plata* Chardonnay, and I'll need a list of the most prominent Caribbean-themed restaurants in Philadelphia and Washington to start."

His mind still reeling, he stood up, pushing away from her desk, feeling hurried and unsettled. "Of course." Should he thank her? For the promotion that he wasn't certain he wanted? It seemed like the right thing to do etiquette-wise. "Uh, thank you, Alice."

"No." She looked up at him, her eyes meeting his and holding them. "You took a chance on me when no one else would. Thank *you*, Carlos."

After a very brief upward tilt of her lips, she turned back to her monitor, her fingers flying across the keyboard as she began working.

And Carlos, who had just received a career-changing promotion, tried to reconcile his warring feelings as he headed back to his desk with heavy steps.

Chapter 5

That evening, as Carlos packed his suitcase for tomorrow's trip, he couldn't stop thinking about the conversation he'd had in Alice's office.

It was hours later, and his feelings were *still* all over the place.

Part of him was grateful for her confidence in him.

Part of him was proud that he had such an opportunity available to him.

But most of him was increasingly annoyed with the way Alice had made the decision for him without waiting for him to accept or decline her offer.

As he folded his T-shirts carefully, he mumbled, his proper English taking a dive as he articulated his feelings "You know what? I never said I *wanted* a promotion. I'm still on the fence about grad school, *por Dios*. How 'bout you stop steamrollin' me and let me make my own decisions in my own time, eh?"

He sighed with annoyance, picking up the snow-white shirts and placing them into the corner of his rolling suitcase, then adding six carefully rolled pairs of khaki-colored socks. Since they'd be in the Caribbean in August, where it would be hella hot, he'd decided to eschew business suits and ties for khaki pants with long-sleeved oxford dress shirts. He wished he could add sandals to his more casual attire as well, but he knew that would be taking it a step too far. No way would Alice be wearing sandals. She'd be in heels, as always.

"Loosen that hair a little and let the blood flow. You too uptight. I don't mean no disrespect, because you know how I feel 'bout you, *querida*, but…" He stopped talking, his hands freezing over the small, neat pile of socks as he let the spoken stream of consciousness suck all the air out of his room.

Fuck. There it was.

You know how I feel about you, querida.

You know *how I feel about you.*

And yet, she didn't.

Not at all.

She didn't know that most of his best dreams featured her.

She didn't know that of every woman in the world, he admired her the most.

She didn't know that asking him to stop working directly for her was painful for him.

She didn't know anything.

"Because you never say nothin'," he murmured, straightening up and putting his hands on his hips as he sucked his lower lip into his mouth. He took a deep breath, then sighed. "What'm'I s'posed to say?"

Shaking his head, he pivoted back to his dresser and pulled out seven pairs of black boxer briefs, throwing them on the bed to be refolded before he packed them. Reaching for the first pair, he folded them in thirds, then in half, setting them to the side.

"What? Like…I have a thing for you? A crush?" He

grimaced, feeling irritated. "Nah. You can't do that. She's your boss, *pendejo*. She don't wanna to hear that from you."

He folded another pair. Then another.

When we return from Puerto Rico, you'll be promoted to Shane's group and given a commensurate raise.

He growled softly, finishing the fourth pair.

"No, thank you," he said, using proper English. "I'm happy where I am, Alice. I like being the office manager. I like helping out Shane with the Latin American clients. I like—Fuck."

He sighed again, folding number five.

"I *like* being with you. I *like* working with you. I *like* seeing you every day—*fifty times* every day. And…"

He grabbed number six, making the creases tight.

"And if you wanna to know the truth, I'll tell it to you: I don't want nobody else takin' care of you," he said. "I don't want nobody else gettin' your coffee or answerin' your phones or runnin' your office, 'cause I know they ain't gonna to care 'bout *it*—and *you*—like *I* care. So, no, *cariño*, you're not promotin' me to Shane's team, *entiendes*? You're not movin' me somewhere else. Know why? 'Cause *I* take care of you, Allie. *Me*. That's what *I* do. And not just 'cause it's my job but—"

Ring. Ring.

His voice cut off, and Carlos snapped his head up from folding the final pair of underwear.

Ring. Ring.

Someone was at the door? Huh. Who? He wasn't expecting anyone. He folded the thirds in half and added them to the neat tower.

Ring. Ring.

"*Dios mío*, I'm coming!" he yelled, hurrying down the stairs. "*Calmate!*"

Arriving at the front door, he unlocked and opened it, looking up to find his cousin Lena standing on the stoop outside, a sour expression on her face.

"Hey, Lena!" he said, reaching out to hug her. *"Que paso?"*

She allowed him to embrace her but didn't hug him back, pulling away to sidestep around him into his apartment. She stood with her back to him for a long moment before turning around.

"My *friends?*" she said, her eyes narrow and furious. "You're fucking around with my friends now, Carlitos?"

Ay, carajo. Just when he'd mostly forgotten about Alicia-Felicia, she was back to bite him in the ass.

"Lena," he said cajolingly, "come on."

"Leticia no es una puta!" Leticia isn't a whore!

"Leticia!" he exclaimed. "That's her name."

Lena crossed her arms over her chest, her eyes popping out of her skull. "Oh, man, you have *got* to be kidding me here. You dogged my friend and you didn't even know her name? *Puerco."* Pig.

He crossed his arms over his chest, mirroring her. "What you want me to say?"

"Thanks for asking," she said, her tone frosty. "I want you to make it right so I don't have to avoid one of my best friends...*or* hear her calling my favorite cousin *un cabrón* every time I turn around."

"Your favorite, huh?" he confirmed, grinning at her.

"You're a cocky piece of shit," she said with attitude. "But, yeah. My favorite."

He winked at her. "How you want me to make it right, *prima?*"

"Ask her out nice. Take her to dinner. Dancing. I don't know. Just fix it so she don't feel like a whore."

"She sorta acts like one," said Carlos, raising an eyebrow.

"*A mi no me importa!*" yelled Lena. "I work with her, Carlos! I see her every goddamned day! She's my friend, and I *vouched* for you on Sunday night. You gotta make it right."

He uncrossed his arms, frowning at her. "Fine. I'll take her to dinner. But not 'til next week. I'm goin' away on business tomorrow."

"Oh, yeah?" asked Lena, her posture finally relaxing. "Where you goin', hotshot?"

"*La Republica,*" he said.

"Wow!" said Lena, grinning at him.

"And home too," he added, grinning back at her.

"*La Isla!* To Toa Baja?"

"Nah. To Ponce. But still…"

"You gonna see *la familia* while you're there?"

"*Espero que sí,*" he answered. *I hope I can.* Though, to be honest, he hadn't really figured it out yet. He'd have to see if there was an afternoon or evening free when he could drive up from Ponce and spend a few hours with his folks. "Hey, you want a beer or something?"

She took her phone out of her back pocket and shook her head. "Nah. I gotta go. I got work in half an hour. I just needed to make sure we talked. You got Leticia's digits?"

Probably not.

She pursed her lips. "I'll send them to you."

"Great," he said as unenthusiastically as possible.

"You don't have to marry her, *pendejo.* Just be nice so she don't feel all weird about you and blame me."

"Yeah, yeah," he said, opening the door for Lena. "I'll take her out. Fine."

"Somewhere nice," said Lena, leaning up on tiptoes to kiss his cheek. "Promise me."

"*Te lo prometo.* Anything else, *mija?*"

"*Te quiero mucho.* Travel safe," she said, kissing his other cheek before heading out the door.

"*Nos vemos, querida,*" he called, pulling the door closed as she headed down the block, back toward *Centro de Oro* and the restaurant where she was a hostess.

As he locked the door, his phone buzzed, and he pulled it from the pocket of his sweat pants to find Lena's text with Alicia-Felicia-Leticia's phone number. He stared at the text as he headed back up the stairs to finish packing.

He had no interest in asking Lena's friend out for dinner.

The only person he *was* interested in was someone he couldn't have.

He pictured Alice. Her cool blonde hair. Her brown eyes. Her designer clothes and fancy education. Her small, perfect tits and pencil-thin body. She was an heiress. His boss. Way, way, *way* out of his league. The closest he was ever going to get to a woman like Alice Story was buying her coffee and answering her phone. The sooner he accepted it, the better.

When we return from Puerto Rico, you'll be promoted to Shane's group and given a commensurate raise. It's for the best…It's done.

Pausing by his suitcase, he opened a new text message and asked Alicia-Felicia-Leticia if she had any time to grab some dinner when he got back from his trip.

***

Alice shot up in bed, gasping, her breath coming in short, shallow, choppy bursts, the only sound in her still-dark bedroom.

"Oh, my God," she panted, covering her heart with her palm and reaching for the glass of water on her bedside table. She took a shaky gulp, whimpering as she replaced the glass and sunk back down under her comforter. "Oh, no."

Her clit was still trembling in soft, orgasmic waves, and she could feel warm moisture pooled in her underwear. She'd had a wet dream. At thirty-*freaking*-three, she'd just had a wet dream.

"For Christ's sake," she muttered, angry with herself, embarrassed and frustrated, though the leftover ripples of pleasure still made her breath catch as her dream came back to her in soft, seductive black and white.

…and gray.

The same gray as his eyes.

"Shit," she whispered, rolling onto her side and pulling her knees to her chest. "Shit…shit…shit, Alice."

She could only remember the dream in shaded bits and pieces, but it had started with her sitting on a garden bench in the mist. The bench was of white stone, cool against her bare skin. She hadn't been naked, but she was wearing a short, thin silk robe. Her legs had been crossed, her eyes closed. The garden had smelled of honey-scented flowers and the sea, a heady mixture of warm salt and sweetness, which she could still smell as she recalled the gentle heaviness of his hands dropping to her shoulders.

She knew it was him, knew that he shouldn't be in her private garden, touching her so intimately, so she hadn't looked up at him, though her body had reveled in his touch.

Ah-leese…Ah-leese…cariño, he'd whispered near her ear, his breath hot on the side of her throat as his hand smoothed the silk fabric from her shoulders, baring them.

His lips touched her shoulders as the robe fluttered down her arms, leaving her small breasts naked in the silvery-gray moonlight. His hands reached slowly around her, covering her erect nipples with his palm. She leaned into his touch, letting her head fall back as his lips slid along the column of her neck, his tongue darting out to lick the small cove where her throat and collarbone met.

I have wanted this, mi amor…wanted you for so long, he whispered, his lips tickling her sensitive skin as his thumbs and forefingers gently squeezed the puckered, throbbing tips of her breasts.

Reaching up for his head, her eyes still closed, she threaded her fingers through his hair, pulling him closer to her face, turning to lift her lips to his. His kiss was strong and masterful, hungry and persistent, his tongue demanding entrance to her mouth and her lips helpless to resist him. She'd moaned when their tongues touched, the sound breathy and needy, while tiny lightning bolts of pleasure shot from her lips to her hips, the white heat pooling there. His fingers caressed her nipples, which were hard as little stones and greedy for the touch of his lips, for the hot wetness of his tongue licking and sucking. She whimpered with need, a swirling building between her legs as she struggled to turn around and face him.

Drawing away from her mouth, he'd grasped her hips and lifted her easily, spinning her around on the bench and dropping to his knees on the grass between her parted legs. She opened her eyes to find him staring up at her, his light eyes black with passion in the monochrome of his face. His bare chest rose and fell rapidly with hot breath that grazed the skin of her stomach. Holding her eyes, he parted the rest of her robe without permission and let the silk pool on the bench at her hips.

Naked before him, covered only with moonlight, she'd felt a tremor of unease, but he'd cupped her face, forcing her to look at him.

Do you trust me? he'd asked with his eyes.

With my life, she'd answered with hers.

His fingers had skated up the insides of her thighs while he gazed at her unwaveringly, not allowing her to look away. A small gasp escaped her lips as his questing fingers parted the slick folds of her sex, exposing the pulsing bud of her clit to the coolness of the night air. She'd sucked in a ragged breath as he lowered his head, his tongue landing with practiced perfection on her throbbing flesh.

Carlos, she'd whimpered, her hands landing on his bent head, her fingers curling into his black hair as her neck fell back, her eyes gazing up at the starry sky. She'd let him love her, trusting him, needing him, forcing herself to let go, to let someone else be in control, to…to…to…

And then she'd woken up.

As she remembered the erotic details of the dream, she rolled onto her back, her fingers slipping into her damp panties. On the verge of confusing tears, she closed her eyes and pictured his face, stroking herself with increasing pressure as she heard his voice in her head:

More, mi amor. Show me more. Bring yourself to pleasure and don't stop until you shatter. I'm here. I will keep you safe…

His voice was firm and demanding, low and sensual, his accented English telling her what to do. Tears slipped from the corners of her eyes as her hips rocked and lifted. She was helpless to silence him, so she surrendered, letting his voice override the chaos of her mind until she was filled with him. Writhing under the sheets, Alice brought herself to orgasm, riding out the tremors and waves of deep pleasure until they started to fade. And as they did, an increasingly sharp shame started biting at her consciousness.

This is wrong.

"This is wrong," she said aloud, wiping away her tears and whipping the covers from her body. "He's your employee."

She stood abruptly and pulled her silk nightgown over her head, then slipped her debauched panties the rest of the way down her legs. Crossing her bedroom naked, she jerked open her dresser drawer and pulled out cotton underwear and a sports bra. Hooking it quickly, she pulled some black spandex bike shorts from another drawer and drew them up her legs. She stepped onto her treadmill and programmed it for a brutal workout. Her sleepy brain started to clear as her blood pumped furiously, her legs burning in protest.

"What are you *thinking*?" she demanded out loud, clenching her jaw as sweat started to collect at her temples. "Why are you letting this *happen*?"

If it wasn't already too late, she'd call him and tell him the trip was off. She'd transfer him to Shane's group first thing in the morning. She'd train his replacement herself.

But it was too late.

The vintners at *Bahía de Plata* were waiting to welcome them. Ramirez was expecting them. The trip was happening. It was too late to cancel, and besides, canceling because she was unable to control her subconscious fantasies about a subordinate? That was her problem. No one else's. And it was up to her to figure out—fast—how to manage it.

But how? Could she help the way she felt? Could she help her attraction to him? Could she help her— goddamnit!—*feelings* for him?

A strangled sound of frustration escaped from her throat.

For *years* she'd worked with Carlos.

For *years* they'd had a highly functional, orgasm-dream-free work relationship.

Why now, *suddenly*, had her brain fixated on him?

"Why *now*?" she cried out, panting with exertion.

The answer—one she truly didn't want—came to her

quickly:

Traveling alone with Carlos had flicked a switch in her brain…but the feelings she was having were too strong not to have existed before this week.

Had she been silently, but desperately, attracted to him for the last three years?

Yes.

Even more than attraction, had she leaned on his care of her, of her business, of her office, of her staff?

Yes.

He had, in some ways—*many* ways—been taking care of her since the day she'd stepped up on her desk in defiance of her father.

Had working so closely with him allowed her to foster an intimacy with him that her brain had sanctioned as appropriate?

Probably.

And had the notion of traveling together been the key that opened the door to her feelings? What *were* her feelings?

Her finger moved to the control panel of the treadmill, steepening the incline of the machine.

Her feelings were…

"Fuck," she murmured breathlessly, out of easy answers.

…more than coworkers, more than gratitude, more than admiration, more than reliance, different from friendship and much more than accord. In fact, Carlos Vega was the only man in the world whom she trusted implicitly, with whom she was her most vulnerable self without fear or reservations.

Oh, God. When had that happened?

Coupled with the way her body still trembled at the thought of her dream, she felt her heart throb, leading her perilously close to uncovering an emotion that Alice hadn't felt for a man in many years.

"No," she growled, panic making her taste bile at the back of her throat.

In *love* with a coworker? Worse, a subordinate? She shook her head, reaching up to swipe away more hot, uncharacteristic tears. "Absolutely not. You may *not* do this. You may *not* fall in love with him, Alice!"

Her phone buzzed loudly from her bedside table, and she pressed the stop button on the treadmill and crossed the room to look at the text:

PRIS: *Up early with Kaitlyn and Theo and wanted to tell you to HAVE FUN! Remember, big sister, he's hot, established, rich, and well educated. Let down your hair and GO FOR IT!*

Alice gulped, staring at the glowing words.

"Ramirez," she murmured, her lips tightening as she lifted her chin.

He *was* good-looking.

He *was* established.

He *was* rich and well educated.

And if she was in the market for a boyfriend, he was an *infinitely* more appropriate match for her than her coworker and subordinate, seven years her junior.

"Ramirez," she said again, this time with more conviction. "Yes. Stop these ridiculous fantasies and choose him instead."

ALICE: *You're right. I will. I will go for it!*

Opening a fresh e-mail, she pulled up Eduardo Ramirez's address and wrote him a quick message, sharing how much she was looking forward to seeing him again.

Then pulling her bra over her head as she stood up, she headed into the bathroom to take a shower and start getting ready for her trip.

Chapter 6

Sitting side by side in the back of a black Cadillac sedan on the way to the airport, Carlos tried not to mind that Alice had barely said "Good morning" before crossing her legs away from him and focusing all her attention on her phone.

He wondered what was so utterly fascinating to her that had her typing out many short messages (Texts? But Alice rarely texted anyone but her sisters!) on her phone and making little giggling (Giggling? Alice Story did not. Fucking. Giggle.) noises every few seconds. Finally, she sighed, placing her phone facedown on her lap, resting her elbow on the gray leather windowsill and watching the rainy morning pass by with a dreamy (Dreamy? Alice was grounded, not a dreamer!) expression on her face.

"Busy morning?" he asked.

"Quite," she answered, still looking out the window.

"Did you have breakfast?"

"Mmm," she murmured.

"I wouldn't mind getting something at the airport," he said, wishing she'd turn and face him so he could read her eyes.

The phone in her lap buzzed, and like a Pavlov puppy, she flipped it over, just out of his glance, and drew it to her face. Her lips twitched, as they occasionally did when she wanted to smile, and she typed out a few words before placing the phone back on her lap.

His eyes followed the movement, which drew his glance to her exposed thigh.

She was wearing a navy-blue suit this morning, sharp and tailored, with a short skirt that rose up quite a bit while she was seated. For once, maybe because she anticipated a warmer climate upon their arrival in the Dominican Republic, she wasn't wearing panty hose. Her legs were smooth as silk, and his mouth watered a little as he gazed at them.

Scowling, he turned away from her, looking out his own window.

"Then you should," she said.

"Should?"

"Get something to eat at the airport."

He *should* take the promotion.

He *should* move to Shane's group.

He *should* get something to eat at the airport.

She should stop telling him what to do!

"*Mierda*," he muttered.

"Pardon?"

"Nothing."

Her phone buzzed again, and his eyes were drawn, again, to her goddamn legs—*who's the* real *Pavlov puppy here, pendejo?*—which he shouldn't be staring at but couldn't help checking out. Alice was a few years older than him, but she kept herself in damn good shape, exercising regularly. He knew this because she often mentioned taking notes and calls while on her treadmill at home. Suddenly, he had a vision of her running—her face slick with sweat, her small breasts kept in place with a black sports bra. Did she wear a shirt while she ran, or just a bra? Was her stomach as taut as he imagined?

"Ha!" she exclaimed softly, and Carlos slid his eyes up to her face, watching her eyes sparkle as she grinned at her phone before typing a response.

What or who was making her smile and giggle and sigh like this?

His eyes widened and his heart dropped.

Was she seeing someone? No. No, no, no. He'd *know*...wouldn't he?

Her face was softer than usual in profile, as though she'd recently let off some tension—*physically*, maybe—and he wondered if the person who she was writing to was somehow responsible. It made his heart beat faster. Not in a good way.

"Your phone's busy this morning," he observed darkly.

For the first time since she'd gotten into the car, she looked at him squarely, and her cheeks instantly colored, as he imagined they would if he'd caught her in the act of doing something shocking. She cleared her throat and dropped his eyes quickly, her fingers clenching around her phone as she looked out the window again.

"So?"

"*Real* busy," he said, rubbing his lower lip with his index finger, feeling annoyed, like he wanted to punch someone—the someone responsible for her texts and giggles.

She took a deep breath but otherwise didn't acknowledge his comment.

"One of your sisters?" he asked hopefully.

She looked at him over her shoulder and down her

nose. "Not that it's any of your business, Carlos, but no. It's not one of my sisters."

He raised his chin, holding her eyes, watching as the flush in her cheeks deepened. "A man?"

"I…" She blinked at him, then turned back toward the window. "Yes."

One word. Like a dagger through his heart. Yes.

Fuck.

He turned back to his own window and clenched his teeth until it strained his jaw. He tried to keep his words light. "You've been holding out. I didn't know you had a boyfriend."

"I didn't say I did."

His face whipped to the left to look at her, then accusingly at her phone. "Then who's—?"

"Just because we're traveling together," she said, a little extra steel in her tone, "doesn't give you the right to interrogate me about my personal life. How would you like it?"

"I'd like it fine. Ask me anything," he said.

"Very well. Do *you* have a girlfriend?"

She asked this with a fair amount of attitude, almost like the question was rhetorical.

What had he done, exactly, to be in the doghouse with her? After their conversation yesterday in her office, he'd thought that the air was cleared between them, but ever since she'd gotten in the car today, she'd been avoiding him again. And every time she looked at him and met his eyes, her cheeks bloomed like a hot-pink *flor de maga*. What in the world had happened between then and now, he wondered, to make her behave like this?

"See?" she asked, mistaking his silence for reticence. "You don't like it either."

"No, I don't mind at all. I'll answer," he said, shifting his body so that he faced her. "The truth is…I'm working on it."

"On one girlfriend…or a dozen?"

She looked so saucy, he grinned at her. "What do you know about my girlfriends, Alice?"

Her phone buzzed in her lap, but—*gracias a Dios*—she ignored it, uncrossing her legs, then recrossing them to face him. "You're not the *only* observant one. We used to work back to back, remember?"

"Vividly."

"When you were on your cell phone, it was inches from my ear."

So she'd been listening? To his conversations? But wait…

"I thought you didn't speak Spanish."

"Well," she said, looking up at him from under lowered lashes, her expression almost impish, "I *do* speak French…and French and Spanish aren't *so* different. I could make out the—ahem—gist of things."

He chuckled softly, rubbing his chin, enjoying her chagrin. "Which was?"

"A lot of girls wanted your attention."

And yet it was only captivated by one, he thought, looking deeply into her eyes, wondering if a day would ever—*could* ever—come when he'd be able to say something like that out loud to her.

"*Sí*," he said lightly, "but none of them has caught me yet."

"But you want to be caught?"

He flinched, his smile slipping. Quickly, he reminded himself that she wasn't asking for herself. "What do you mean?"

"You just said…the one you're working on," she said.

"Ahh. Her. She's going to be…a challenge."

"I see," she said softly, her lips turning down just a touch. Then, suddenly, her eyes brightened. "So that would be a no? You don't, presently, have a girlfriend?"

He stared at her, half-smiling, and she stared back at him, half-smiling as well, when her phone buzzed again. Carlos looked down at it deliberately, then slowly raised his eyes to hers, letting his gaze track the curves of her breasts behind her suit jacket.

"Don't you need to write back?" he asked, his voice soft and low. "He'll think you don't care."

"You haven't answered my question yet," she murmured, and he realized that her chest was rising and falling faster than it was a few seconds before.

"Does it matter?"

"I…" she started. Her tongue darted out to lick her lips, and his eyes dropped to her mouth, staring at it hungrily, watching as she whispered, "It shouldn't."

His heart, which had stuttered at the sight of her tongue, now launched into a feverish gallop. What did she mean? What did *that* mean? That it *did* matter? That she *cared* whether or not he was single? He jerked his eyes to hers, searching them for answers.

"*Does it*, Ah-leese?" he asked, feeling sick and stricken, hopeful and stunned.

Her phone buzzed in her lap again, and she jumped slightly, blinking at him as though coming out of a dream. She exhaled deeply, like she'd been holding her breath, and slid her eyes from his, turning over the phone and looking down at her new messages.

When she looked back up at him, her expression was cooler, her smile gone.

"No," she said gently, and if he wasn't mistaken, a little sadly. "You're my employee. It's none of my business."

There it was: Alice's wall.

And a good reminder to Carlos that she would never, ever see him as dating material, as someone she could be with, as someone she could date or kiss or sleep with or love. No. He was her employee—at best, her coworker—and in her mind, he was absolutely, positively off-limits.

Unable to bear the crushing disappointment he felt, he shifted away from her, turning back to the window as they exited the highway and entered the airport.

***

After they got through security, Carlos had curtly informed her that he was going to go have some breakfast and would meet her at the gate. Alice had nodded, sorry for the frostiness between them and blaming herself for it.

It shouldn't? Goddamn it, Alice. It shouldn't?

She still couldn't believe those words had issued from her mouth.

It was bad enough that she'd engaged in banter about him having a girlfriend, but when he'd stared into her eyes, then exchanged them for a starving glance at her lips, she'd been mesmerized. Her sex dream had come rushing back to her, and before she could stop herself, she'd said it:

It shouldn't.

The unspoken part of her words, obviously, that *it did*.

It mattered. It ate her up to think of him with someone else. It was probably why she'd kept their personal lives so strictly separate all these years, not because of propriety, but because she didn't know how she'd bear to see him with another woman. The mere thought squeezed her heart like a vise, making it hard for her to breathe.

Did she know that Carlos—well—got around? Yes.

Yes, of course. She wasn't lying when she said she'd heard many a whispered conversation that included words like "*querida*," "*muñeca*," and "*cariño*." She'd Googled the words as fast as he'd said them, and she'd gotten the picture early on: Carlos Vega was a player.

But it hadn't hurt her. In those days, she'd viewed his dalliances with an inner eye roll and an affectionate shake of her head. She had felt affection for him, of course, but it was reined in and appropriate. Now? Were she to hear him talking to a "*querida/muñeca/cariño*," it would roll her stomach instead of her eyes and make her fingernails break the skin on her palms.

When had things changed? When had her feelings for him become so possessive? And why hadn't she noticed sooner?

Maybe because they didn't sit back to back anymore. She didn't have to hear him on the phone with his *nenes*. Or maybe, at some point, he'd stopped talking to them at the office. That was possible too.

Who was this girl, she wondered, whom he'd referenced in the car? This "challenging" girl that he was working on?

Did she realize the man she was getting? That he was loyal and trustworthy, caring and kind? Did she know that he said yes more than no? That he was the type of man who remembered your favorite drink and food and restaurant and spa and hotel? Did this challenging girl know that when he laughed, his cheeks dented because his dimples were so deep? And that his eyelashes practically fanned his cheeks when he blinked? Did she notice that his careful English slipped a little as the day wore on and that he occasionally peppered his speech with Spanish? Did she know how smart he was? How fast he picked up new skills? That he only needed to hear a name once and he'd remember it forever? Did she know how extraordinary he was? Did she care?

Alice looked up to see she'd arrived at her gate and checked her watch as she took a seat. Twenty minutes until boarding. Twenty minutes to think about how much she wished she could be—even for a few precious moments in time—the challenging girl that Carlos wished would love him.

Suddenly, before her, a Starbucks cup appeared, and she reached for it as she looked up to see Carlos smiling down at her.

"They didn't have iced, so I got your second favorite."

"My…?"

"Caffè latte," he said. "With nutmeg and cinnamon."

My second favorite.

Oh, my heart.

"I'm sorry," she murmured.

"For what?"

"For making things uncomfortable between us in the car. I had no right to ask you personal questions."

He sat down beside her, opening a paper sack and removing a toasted bagel. "It doesn't bother me to share my personal life with you, Allie."

"What?"

"I said I don't mind sharing—"

"No," she said, staring at him with a bit of wonder. Only her sister had ever called her "Allie" and only for a very short period of time when she was younger. It felt strange—and somehow perfect—for Carlos to call her by that nickname. "What did you call me?"

He searched her eyes for a moment before his lips parted in understanding. "Oh. Sorry."

"You called me Allie."

He sighed, taking a bite of his bagel. "I won't do it again."

"I don't mind," she said quickly.

She gave him a small smile, then took a sip of her coffee.

"Okay," he said slowly, nodding at her before taking another bite of his bagel.

"My sisters called me Allie when I was younger."

"Yeah, I know."

"*How* do you know?" she asked, elbowing him playfully in the side. "You weren't there."

He grimaced at her, rubbing his side like she'd hurt him. "You know I see all your e-mails, right? I mean…I *can*. I have access."

"You read my e-mails?" she gasped, thinking about the overtly flirtatious messages that she and Eduardo had exchanged this morning.

"No," he said. "Of course not. Not regularly. But at times you've asked me to find a name or address, and so I've had to go back through your correspondence to look for it."

"And…?"

"And when you, Margaret, and Priscilla were trading e-mails about the Five Sisters Vineyard, I noticed that Priscilla sometimes addressed you as 'Allie.' That's all."

Her shoulders lowered, and she blew out a breath. "You know a lot about me."

He took another bite of bagel and nodded. "Mm-hm."

"Why don't you want the promotion?" she asked, remembering his face in her office yesterday and knowing instinctively that he wasn't as decided about it as she was.

"I never said I didn't."

"You're not the only one who's observant," she said. "You weren't exactly clapping your hands together with glee when I said I was promoting you."

He took a final bite of bagel, then stuffed the rest back into the paper bag, rubbing the poppy seeds from his hands as he finished chewing.

She got the feeling that he was stalling—that he didn't want to answer. But Alice knew from experience that if she stayed quiet, he would.

He swallowed, then reached down for his blue Gatorade and took a sip.

"Why don't you want it?" she asked again.

"I don't know," he said, looking away from her as the gate agent announced that they were about to start the early boarding process. He stood up and extended the handle on his suitcase. "We should get in line."

She looked up at him, wondering why in the world he would choose to stay in a lower management position when something more lucrative and challenging was being offered to him. It didn't make sense to her. It defied reason. Ergo, it must be personal, and she had no right to pry into his personal reasons for not wanting more responsibility.

"Carlos," she said. He looked down at her, his gray eyes soft. "Will you tell me when you're ready?"

His eyes were locked with hers, and for just a moment—a split second—she wondered if it was possible that there wasn't actually a major reason for him to share. If, in fact, he just liked his job and didn't want to move. If, perhaps, he had so little ambition that staying in a static position forever would be okay with him. She felt her eyebrows furrow and the crease between them deepen. Alice had never known anything but clawing her way to get ahead in a "man's" world. What would it be like to stop? To realize that what she had was enough? To make time for more than work and business in her life? She could barely fathom it.

"Sure, Allie," he said, tilting his head to the side as he extended the handle on her rolling suitcase and offered it to her.

She stood up and preceded him to the jetway, her thoughts conflicted and complicated as she offered her boarding pass to the gate agent and found her business-class row. Suddenly she felt exhausted: tired from waking up so early, weary from fighting her feelings and wondering about his. All she really wanted to do was close her eyes for a little while.

"Champagne, ma'am?" asked the flight attendant as Carlos lifted their suitcases into the overhead bin and Alice took the seat by the window. "Sir?"

"No, thank you," said Alice, looking up at Carlos. "I think I'll catch up on sleep, if that's okay."

"Of course," he said, taking the seat beside her. "I'll wake you up when we get there."

***

Halfway through the flight, they'd encountered a bit of turbulence, and though Alice had slept through it, her head had fallen onto Carlos' shoulder.

And now, about forty minutes from landing in Santo Domingo, he held himself as still as possible, cherishing the soft weight of her resting head, breathing in the scent of her light floral shampoo, and wishing that they were flying to Brazil or somewhere even further instead.

The last few days had proven eye opening for Carlos in so many ways, it was hard for him to get his head around them, but hardest of all to assimilate was when she'd gazed at him across the back seat of that Cadillac earlier today and told him that "it shouldn't" matter to her if he was available or taken.

It was the closest Alice had ever come to expressing

feelings for him that had nothing to do with gratitude or loyalty. And although it had angered him when she'd tried to verbally negate the words a few seconds later, he'd never forget them. Because "it shouldn't" meant it did.

It mattered to her.

He'd figured this out as he stood behind her in the line for security and bought himself a bagel for breakfast. In fact, it was why he'd softened, picking up something for her too.

It didn't matter that he was her employee.

It didn't matter that he was younger than she.

Somewhere inside of Alice Story, she *cared* for him, and not just as a coworker, but in the way a woman cares for a man.

She just didn't want to…or think she should.

And there it was again: that *pendejo* "should" that kept getting in their way.

She murmured in her sleep, nestling closer to him, and he turned his head a fraction of an inch and closed his eyes, touching the top of her head with his lips in a sweet, soft, forbidden kiss.

When he opened his eyes, he looked out the window at the bright-blue Caribbean below and reminded himself that he had a week with Alice—he might never have that again and he needed to make it count.

He would take care of her this week, just as he'd always done, but maybe he could also help her understand that if two consenting adults wanted to be with each other, where they worked, where they came from, or the age on their birth certificates didn't matter.

He pressed his lips to her crown one last time before straightening wistfully.

All that mattered was blasting that fucking "should" out of the equation so that the path to one another was cleared.

And then?

Then they'd find out what exactly had been growing strongly and silently between them all these years spent together.

Chapter 7

It was apparent, from the moment they exited customs, that Alice wasn't in Kansas anymore.

And Carlos was in his element.

From the way he flirted with the homely, portly immigration official, somehow fast-tracking them to the front of the line, to the way the way he joked with the customs officers, calling them all "papi" and high-fiving them before they proceeded seamlessly to baggage claim, Alice was quickly learning why Shane had praised Carlos' skills while traveling together in Latin America.

Back in Philadelphia, he walked tall, with a certain confidence and swagger, yes.

But it turned out that he was actually being reserved at home.

Here? In the Caribbean?

He was a walking, talking charmer. A living and breathing Don Juan. And a beyond-perfect travel companion, somehow managing to move them to the front of the car rental line and getting them upgraded from a Toyota to a BMW.

As they walked over to the sleek black car, Alice looked

up at him, shaking her head. "You're a man of hidden talents."

He chuckled softly. "Maybe."

"No, really," she said. "I've never seen anyone work an airport like that. It was almost as if you sprinkled the whole place with fairy dust."

He raised an eyebrow at her. "*Fairy* dust?"

"Proverbially."

"If I was less confident in my sexuality, I might take offense."

"Oh, give me a break!" she guffawed. "You ooze—"

Oh, God.

She was about to say "sex appeal."

She could feel her cheeks flare with heat as she rolled her suitcase to the truck of the car and stopped.

"Alice Story," he said from behind her, his voice holding back barely restrained laughter, "what were you about to say?"

She turned to face him, lifting her chin despite her chagrin. "I don't need to say it. You know exactly how charming you are."

He rolled his suitcase next to hers and slid his hands into his pockets. "I don't. You'll have to enlighten me."

He looked so cool and cocky, a delicious shiver rolled down her back and the breath she drew was slightly ragged.

"You're a terrible flirt," she said softly, her voice lacking real conviction. Damn him for being so effortlessly smooth and devastatingly handsome.

"No, Allie," he said, his gray eyes dark and wide as he looked down at her. "Back there? I was just being myself. When I start flirting with someone…you'll know."

He lifted one of his hands, and Alice's breath caught, some part of her certain he was going to raise his palm to her cheek and cup it. Draw her closer. Let his lips drop to hers. Would she stop him if he tried something like that? Would she have the strength to push him away?

A high-pitched *beep-beep* noise made her jump as she realized that he'd just taken the keys out of his pocket and unlocked the trunk.

She blinked at him, discomposed. "You opened the trunk."

"Yes, boss." He grinned at her. "Were you expecting something else?"

"Nope!" she chirped. "That's, um, perfect. Because…bags. I'm—I'm going to go and, um, sit in the car."

"Okay."

His lips were tilted up in a knowing smile, and she turned away from him abruptly, marching around the car to the passenger side and opening the door. Easing herself into the hot interior, she sat down and settled herself, unbuttoning and shrugging out of her hot suit jacket, which she draped over the back seat. Wearing only a white silk tank top, she leaned back against the supple leather seat, waiting for him to join her and turn on the air conditioning.

She heard the trunk slam shut, and a moment later the driver's door opened. He slid into his seat, looking over at her.

"You took off your jacket."

"I didn't expect it to be so hot," she sighed.

He nodded, his eyes dropping to the arm closest to him for a second. "You never take off your jacket."

"It's not this hot in Philadelphia," she said, suddenly feeling a little self-conscious as he inspected her bare arm. Reaching into her bag for an elastic, she gathered her shoulder-length hair in her hand and fastened it into a high ponytail.

He watched her with an intensity bordering on fascination, his eyes darkening as she smoothed some flyaway strands of blonde behind her ears. "What?"

"I like your—" He gestured to her ponytail with a soft chuckle. "It's cute."

Cute? Of all the words she'd heard from men to describe her looks, cute generally didn't make the list. Striking? Stunning? Gorgeous? Yes. Cute? No. But as he grinned at her, she found herself smiling back, because this was Carlos, and a genuine "cute" from him was worth a hundred contrived compliments from other men.

"Thank you," she said.

"You're right," he said, "it's hot."

He leaned forward, the muscles in his shoulders bunching and twisting as he shrugged out of his own jacket, laying it in the back seat on top of hers. She watched as he unbuttoned the cuffs of his starched, long-sleeved, white buttoned-down shirt, then rolled the sleeves halfway up his forearms.

Since he rarely removed his jacket, she wasn't accustomed to seeing the veins that twisted up his tanned skin or the muscle tone in his forearms that was hidden from her on a daily basis. She suddenly wondered what he did for exercise to make his arms so muscular.

He cleared his throat, and she snapped her eyes up from his arm, blinking up at him before facing front.

"The islands are always humid," he said, putting the key in the ignition and turning over the powerful engine. He fiddled with the controls, and air conditioning suddenly blasted from the vents, making goose bumps stand up on Alice's arms. "Have you ever been to the Caribbean?"

She shook her head, still not trusting herself to look his

way without ogling his toned arms again. "No. My parents didn't take us on many vacations, but when they did, it was exclusively to Europe."

"You missed out."

"How do you mean?" she asked as he backed out of the rental car parking space and pointed them toward the airport exit.

"It's a beautiful world down here," he said, reaching forward to turn on the radio. "Look around, Allie."

As some gentle, rhythmic music filled the car, she rolled down her window, letting the warm breeze kiss her bare neck. As she looked out the windshield to the left, she was startled by the sparkling electric blue of the sea.

"Ohhhh," she murmured.

"Pretty spectacular, eh? *El mar*," said Carlos, looking out his window before shooting her a perplexed look. "Your window's down."

She nodded. "Uh-huh."

"But the AC's on."

"Uh-huh."

"You're a woman of contradictions, Alice."

"How so?" she asked, crossing her legs toward him as he stared straight ahead at the palm tree–lined highway.

She could observe him like this—while they were conversing and he was driving—without seeming like a lecherous cougar. She traced the strong line of his square jaw, the bristle of his jet-black beard just starting to grow in after a day of travel, his omnipresent dimples, deeper when he was amused, and those long, long lashes that made his gray eyes look so sweet, so innocent, when his body was clearly made for wickedness.

Her cheeks flushed as her thoughts took a dive, but she didn't look away from him. First of all, he wasn't looking her way, but second of all, he'd caught her blushing so many times this week, what did it matter now anyway?

"You really want to know?" he asked.

She nodded. "I value your opinion."

The dimple closest to her dented his cheek as he grinned her at words.

"Okay," he said. "Well, for starters, you're a tough businesswoman, but you've got a real soft spot for your employees."

"Hmm," she murmured, unable to argue with him. "That's true. What else?"

"Your father did a number on you and your sisters. You could hate him for it, but you don't."

"Sometimes I do," she argued.

"No," he said softly, glancing at her. "You get annoyed by him. Disappointed. Hurt. You don't hate him. I've never seen you hate anyone."

He was right, of course. "What else?"

"You hide…" He stopped, adjusting his hands on the steering wheel.

"I hide?"

He sighed. "You hide behind work, I think, because you don't trust people." He cleared his throat. "Men, especially."

She flinched, her brows pinching together as she watched his face for meanness or judgment but found neither. "What do you mean?"

He glanced at her quickly before looking back at the road. "I've watched a hundred men make passes at you over the years. But you…"

"I what?" she murmured, hanging on his words, hoping he could help her see herself as clearly as he did.

"You have trouble trusting men. *That's* your father's

legacy to you."

Alice was silent as her gaze fell from Carlos' face. "You're right. Trust doesn't...doesn't come easily for me."

Except with you, her heart qualified. *I trust you, Carlos. Of all men on earth, I trust you the most.*

"I understand why," he said gently. "You're an heiress. You own a successful company. Your family name is old and powerful. You worry that a man could pretend to care for you but have ulterior motives."

She nodded, playing with the hem of her skirt as he told her truths about her life that she'd never actually articulated aloud.

"But someday," he said, a certainty to his voice that made her fragile hopes turn to yearning, "a man might come along who doesn't care about any of that. A man might come along who just wants you for *you*."

She looked up at him, surprised by the sudden and unexpected burn of tears at the back of her eyes. She clenched her jaw, willing herself not to cry.

Carlos stopped at a red light and turned to her, his gray eyes soft yet still intense. "I hope when he does, you'll be able to see him."

She gazed back at him, wondering, *Are you that man? Could you be that man for me? You, who followed me when I couldn't offer you anything except a promise? You, who gave me your trust when I hadn't earned it? You, who invade my dreams and make my heart tremble with longing? You, younger than me yet somehow wiser than me, filling spaces in my heart that I didn't realize were empty?*

The car behind them honked to let them know the light had changed, and suddenly his words from earlier circled back to her: *I'm working on it. She's going to be...a challenge.*

Smarten up, Alice.

He *had* someone in his life whom he was pursuing. And

it certainly wasn't his seven-years-older, complicated, demanding, workaholic boss.

She sighed.

"Me too," she said, reaching forward to turn up the radio, rest her elbow on the open window, and watch sun-kissed Santo Domingo slide quickly by.

***

An hour later they checked in at the *Gran Palacio de Plata* and were taken, via golf cart, to their adjoining rooms, which overlooked the Caribbean. Evening was quickly approaching, and it was too late for a tour of the vineyards, though they'd been promised one first thing in the morning.

As the golf cart sped away, Alice turned to Carlos.

"Travel is always tiring," she said, pressing her key card to the reader. "See you in the morning?"

"How about an early dinner?" he asked quickly.

"Dinner?" she parroted, her eyes widening like he'd asked her out on a hot date.

"We have to eat, right?"

"I guess so."

"And I'm sure there are some local wines served at the restaurant, so we could try one. Be ready for tomorrow."

"Of course," she said. "Good idea."

He twisted his wrist and looked at his watch. "It's five now. Why don't we give ourselves an hour to unpack and freshen up?"

"Okay. Yes," she said, nodding at him as she pushed her room door open. "Sounds good."

"I'll see you here in an hour."

He watched her go, waiting until her door was closed and latched before letting himself inside of his room.

He pulled his suitcase to the bed and flopped down on his back, staring up at the ceiling fan, which rotated in lazy circles.

From their charged conversation in the car, to making up at the airport, to the soft weight of her sleeping head on his shoulder, to their discussion in the drive from Santo Domingo, he could *feel* things changing between them. And because he *wanted* the change—*embraced* it, even—he could only hope that working with each other had built a foundation strong enough to sustain it.

He could see her fighting herself as they drew closer, the way she'd lean a little closer to him, then force herself to jerk back. Lean closer, jerk back. What would it take, he wondered, for her to keep leaning? For her to trust that she could lean closer? Lean *on* him? That he was strong enough for both of them personally the way she'd been strong enough for them professionally.

He turned on the TV and unpacked three days' worth of clothes, then took a quick shower, shaving and dressing in jeans and a light-blue buttoned-down dress shirt, which he rolled to the elbows. Chuckling softly as he remembered her staring at his arms in the car, he made a mental note to only wear a jacket if they were actually attending a business meeting and let his body tempt her whenever else possible.

At five fifty-eight, he stepped outside his door to wait for her.

A moment later, she appeared, wearing a simple navy-blue dress with a V neck and a white sweater thrown over her arm. She'd brushed out her blonde hair and put it back in a hairband, a style she didn't wear very often, but it made her look younger than the tight bun she generally favored.

"You look nice," he said, grinning at her.

"You too," she said, glancing down at his pants. "I don't think I've ever seen you in jeans."

"Do you mind?"

She shook her head. "Of course not. This isn't a business meeting. Just a—a casual dinner. Between coworkers."

"Shall we?" he asked, gesturing toward the restaurant at the back of the main resort building.

They walked mostly in silence, as though accustoming themselves to each other out of the office. The path to the resort was lined with frangipani, and Carlos breathed deeply, savoring the smell of the sweet tropical blooms mixed with the brackish air from the sea.

"It's lovely, isn't it?" asked Alice, nodding toward the ocean.

He smiled. "Sí. It reminds me of home."

"You miss it?"

"I miss my family." He paused as his bare arm brushed against hers, and his voice deepened as he added, "But I made the right choice to move to Philly."

They reached the entrance to an open-air restaurant, and Carlos gestured for her to precede him onto the small patio, which had tiki torches lining the perimeter and lit candles on every table.

"*Dos para cenar?*" asked the hostess.

"*Sí, gracias,*" answered Carlos. The hostess led them to a two-person table, and Carlos helped Alice with her chair.

A waitress appeared to fill their glasses with ice water.

"Honeymooners?" she asked with a sunny grin and a heavy accent.

"Honeymooners? No!" said Alice, jerking her head to look up at the server. "No. Coworkers. We work together. That's all."

The waitress looked at Alice like she was covered in crazy. "Ah. *Sí. Bueno.*"

Carlos looked up at the waitress and gave her a tight

smile, taken down a little by Alice's vehement denial.

"*Mi suerte, guapo*," she said, grinning back at him. *My luck, handsome.*

Alice cleared her throat, drawing their attention away from each other and back to her. "I'd like some wine, please."

"*Sí*, of course, madam."

"Do you want wine?" Alice asked Carlos, cocking her head to the side. "I don't actually know if you drink it."

"I do," he answered. "You choose."

She requested a bottle of the local *Bahía de Plata* Chardonnay, waited until the waitress sauntered away, then turned to him. "What did she say to you?"

"Huh?"

"The waitress," she clarified, toying with her empty wineglass as spots of pink appeared high on her cheeks.

Is she jealous? he wondered. *Please, Lord, let her be jealous.* Carlos tilted his head to the side, staring at her with a slight smile. "She said that she was in luck."

"Why?"

"I assume because you made it clear that we aren't together."

Alice's eyes flared with heat that Carlos quietly welcomed, taking satisfaction in her reaction. "Oh."

"Mmm," he hummed, leaning forward. "But I'm not interested in her."

"N-No?"

"Nope." He shook his head. "I'm not ready to give up on my challenge yet."

"Right." Her shoulders slumped. "The challenging girl you're working on."

Carlos nodded slowly, holding her eyes, wondering if any part of Alice knew that he was talking about her.

The waitress returned with their wine, offering the bottle to Carlos for inspection. But he shook his head, gesturing to Alice. "*Dáselo a ella.*" For her.

"*La señora?*" The lady?

"*Sí. Porque no?*" Sure. Why not?

"*Bueno.*" She shifted, showing the bottle to Alice instead.

"Looks perfect. Thank you," said Alice, though she was looking at Carlos, not the waitress.

As the server poured the wine in their glasses and then iced it in a small silver bucket tableside, a four-man band, wearing *ponchos campesinos,* entered the patio and set themselves up on a small stage in the corner behind Carlos.

"Cheers," said Alice, raising her glass.

"What are we toasting?" he asked.

"Caribbean wines," she said, offering him a rare smile.

He grinned back at her, clinking her glass before letting the smooth, buttery Chardonnay slide down his throat.

"What do you think?" she asked.

"Good. *Very* good."

"I agree," she said, holding onto her glass as she looked over at the musicians. "Is this Caribbean music?"

Carlos followed her eyes over his shoulder. "No. South American. See the guy on the right? He's playing a *zamponia*. A pan flute. It's not typically Caribbean."

"I like it," she said. "It's unusual."

He shrugged, looking back at Alice. "I guess. I had an aunt from Bolivia, and she used to listen to this kind of music all the time."

As they sipped their wine, a nearby couple stood from their table and started dancing.

Carlos turned to her. "Do you dance, Alice?"

"Me? Not much."

"Do you know how?"

"We all had to learn." She chuckled softly. "I can fox-trot and waltz very poorly."

"For a woman," he said, looking into her eyes across the candlelit table, "dancing isn't as much about skill as it is about trusting her partner. If *he* can lead well, *she* can dance well."

"How are you at leading?" she asked, her voice soft and breathy.

"The best," he said, cocking his head to the side and deciding to take a chance. "Would you like to dance, Allie?"

Her lips parted, and he saw it in her eyes—the instinct to refuse him, to tell him that, no, she didn't want to dance. Would she let her heart, for once, overrule her head? Because the chance to hold her in his arms was so close, he wasn't sure he could stand it if she said no.

"Okay," she said, placing her glass on the table and nodding.

His heart leapt in surprise and elation, and he pushed his chair away from the table, rounding it to help her from her seat. He took her hand in his, flesh against flesh, reveling in the warmth of her skin, the delicate bones underneath. It had been a long time since he'd held her hand—there had been a time or two since he'd helped her down from the desk, to shake on a deal or congratulate her on new business—but this was different. This was completely different.

Pulling her to the small dance floor, he put one arm around her waist, then held up the other for her to clasp. She placed one hand—tentatively, at first—on his shoulder before taking his hand.

For the first time in in three years, Carlos Vega held Alice Story in his arms, and his heart whispered softly, *There's no going back now.*

As they moved together to the soft music, one of the musicians stepped up to the microphone and started to sing:

"Cuando el dulzor de tu mirar, hizo temblar todo mi ser. Cuánta felicidad hallé, saber que tú me amabas también."

"What's he saying?" asked Alice, her voice uncertain, her lips not far from his ear.

His heart skipped a beat as he answered her because the words were terribly romantic, words he'd dreamed of saying to her, though he'd never really imagined he'd have the chance.

"It's a love song," he said. "He said, um…'When the sweetness of your look made me tremble…how much happiness I found to know that you loved me too.'"

He felt her sharp intake of breath as he whispered to her, his breath surely kissing her ear.

"What else?" she asked, the tips of her breasts grazing his shirt as he pulled her closer, entwining his fingers through hers.

He translated for her: "'Everything is beautiful since the moment I loved you. And now, I can never leave you because I adore you so, my darling.'"

"Oh," she murmured softly, her body loosening in his arms, molding more closely to him.

He took their entwined hands, moving hers to his chest and flattening it there, then clasping it with his.

So close now and barely moving beyond a gentle sway, his cheek grazed hers, and he adjusted his hand on her back, holding onto her more tightly, memorizing this moment, lest he should never have the chance to revisit it again.

And Alice, so stalwart and strong and in charge in every other area of her life, leaned on him, *into* him, letting him hold her, letting him guide them, releasing control to him, and—for once—letting someone else be in charge.

The singer continued, and Carlos translated, "'Just when I felt myself dying, the summer of your love arrived. Now I live happy, only for you.'"

Her fingers curled into his shoulder, the words affecting her as deeply as they were him.

"'You taught me how to laugh and how to share. Of so much love, I could almost die. I only live for you,'" he murmured, his lips touching the delicate shell of her ear as they moved easily to the gentle rhythm, their bodies flush and supple.

Desperate to read her expression, he drew back from her just a little as the musicians played a short instrumental interlude, looking down into her eyes, which were wide and dazed. She slid her glance to his lips and rested there.

"Ah-leee," he whispered, wondering if she was inviting him to kiss her.

"Carlos," she whispered, her gaze still fixed hungrily on his lips.

His nose grazed hers, and he felt her breath hitch as she slid her hand from his shoulder to his neck.

He dipped his head to kiss her, then stopped.

Don't do it, warned a sharp voice in his head, piercing the fog of his desire. *I know you want to, but don't do it. It's too soon.*

Flinching with frustrated want, he pulled her close to him, sliding his cheek against hers as the *cantante* started the last verse of the song. The words. Oh, God, the words could have been ripped from his very heart.

This song was written for us, he thought. *For us and nobody else.*

"Tell me the words," she said in his ear, her voice low and breathless.

"'*Cuando me encuentre junto a ti, nunca te apartaré de mi*,'" he sang along with the musicians, whispering against her hair. "'When you're beside me once again, I'll never let you go.'"

She drew a ragged breath, arching her back to be closer to him, her breasts rubbing against his chest with every small movement, her nipples hard through her dress, through his shirt.

"'*Solo sabemos, tú y yo, cuanto sufrimos por este amor...*'" His voice was gritty with emotion as he finished. "'Only we know, you and I, how much we suffer for this love.'"

"Oh," she sighed, the fingers on his chest curling against his shirt as the soft notes of the pan flute floated away on the evening breeze.

Light applause made them still their bodies, and Alice stepped away from him, dropping her hands from his shoulder and neck. She stood facing him, her chest lifting with each breath she took, her eyes stricken as they searched his.

"*Calmate*, Alice," he said gently. "It was just a dance."

She lifted her chin, like she knew he was lying, then turned away from him, heading back to the table and resuming her seat.

His body was in riot, his blood hot with hunger, his skin primed for more of her touch.

Get yourself in check, he thought as he followed her back to the table and sat down across from her.

"This morning," she said, locking her eyes with his, "you said I'd know when you started flirting with someone."

He nodded at her.

"That dance," she said. "You were…flirting. With me."

Was he? Because it felt more like making love to her with their clothes on. But if she needed to call it flirting, he could live with that.

He nodded again. "Yes."

She dropped his eyes, gulping softly as she glanced down at the table before looking back up at him. "It's not a good idea."

"How do you know that?"

"We're impossible, Carlos," she said softly.

"I disagree, Alice."

"We're from different worlds."

"Once, maybe. But the truth is that we've shared the same world for many years now."

"I'm much older than you."

"A few years."

"Seven," she corrected him.

He shrugged. "I don't care."

She paused for a moment as though processing his simple rebuttal, but her eyes were heavy when she finally said, "I'm your boss."

"The best in the world," he replied, nodding.

"Which means it's impossible for us to—"

"No." He leaned forward, reaching for her hand, taking it in his, lacing his strong tan fingers through her delicate white ones. "No, *mi amor*. I won't accept that. Nothing's impossible."

"What about the complicated girl?" she whispered, though her eyes told him she'd finally figured it out.

"I hope she'll give us a chance," he answered, his thumb making soft circles on her hand.

"Please stop," she whispered, pulling her hand away from his, her chest heaving with every breath she took.

"What's next?" asked a chipper voice.

They looked up at the same time to see their waitress standing over them, grinning saucily back and forth between them. "More wine? Dinner?"

Slowly, Carlos slid his eyes from the waitress to Alice.

"What's next, Allie?" he asked her in a low, intimate whisper, his eyes begging her for a chance to see how good they could be together.

"I'm sorry," she blurted out, standing abruptly from her seat and hurrying from the patio.

Chapter 8

Alice set her alarm for five o'clock a.m., hoping to beat the heat by rising early for a run.

When they checked in yesterday morning, she'd asked about running trails and was gratified to learn that while there wasn't a path specifically designated for runners, from one side of the resort to the other was about two miles on a flat, paved trail, and the concierge advised that before seven a.m., it was a runner's paradise.

She tied the laces on her running shoes and stretched her legs, then tucked her room key card in her sports bra as she pulled the door shut behind her.

Purposely looking away from Carlos' room, she turned toward the tennis courts at the west end of the property to find the trailhead, estimating the temperature at about seventy-five degrees. Warm but bearable.

Unlike her memories of last night…which were *hot* and almost *un*bearable.

After leaving the table like a ninny, she'd hidden in her room for the remainder of the evening, pretending to be asleep when Carlos knocked on her door an hour later, telling her that he'd brought her a sandwich for dinner.

It was an unfamiliar role for her—coward—and Alice found she didn't like it at all. But the alternative? Facing him? No thanks.

She'd turned up the air conditioning and buried her sorrows in her pillow.

Her sorrows.

Her *terrible* sorrows.

Only we know, you and I, how much we suffer for this love.

Love.

Is that what this was? Love? This awful ache in her gut and her chest and her head since last night? Because if so, love sucked.

Not that she knew much about it.

I've never been in love, she admitted to herself as she turned the bend and saw the tennis courts up ahead.

Dated? Sure.

Sex? Absolutely.

But love? No.

It had been elusive so far in Alice's life.

But these feelings growing within her were so overwhelming, so overpowering, the only way she could contextualize them was to compare them to how she felt when she had started Alice Story Imports—full of painful hope, able to think of little else, and desperate that she find some satisfaction for the growing need inside of her. At the time, she'd known with little ambiguity that she was in love with her new company and desperate for it to succeed.

But was she in love with Carlos too? Had she fallen in love with him at the same time? Was that how it had started, sharing every step with him along the way? But how dare such feelings manifest themselves when she hadn't given her express permission for such a potent emotion to let loose inside of her?

She reached the trailhead and stretched again, looking at the white-sand beach and aqua-blue ocean to her right. Taking a deep breath, she set forth at a moderate pace, anxious not to overheat as the sun became stronger.

Recognizing the feeling inside of her—even if she was hesitant to name it—was one thing, but coupled with her recent memories of their intimacy last night, it was going to be harder and harder to fight it.

As they'd danced, he'd held her. *Held* her. And she'd never felt so protected or supported in a such a fundamental, physical way—never felt like she could simply close her eyes and let someone else be in charge for a while. It was far more intoxicating than the wine they'd been sharing, this notion that Carlos was strong enough to shoulder some part of her life that she'd neglected so pitifully—namely, romance and love. When it came to relationships and matters of the heart, he was, despite his age, more experienced than she. And regardless of that experience—some of it certainly gratuitous—she knew, in the deepest reaches of her heart, that she could trust him, that he'd never intentionally hurt her.

Running steadily passed the beach on the paved path, she allowed herself to marvel at this amazing fact for just a moment. A man as charming as Carlos, as drop-dead gorgeous, who'd clearly been a player for most of his adult life, was the one man on earth she trusted—and *knew* she could trust—above all others. If she ever gave her heart to him, she knew that it would be safe.

But it didn't matter.

It didn't matter how she felt when he held her, or that she trusted him, or even that they were attracted to one another.

None of it mattered because they were impossible, and

it would be best for both of them if she crushed whatever romantic feelings she had for him and made it clear that his advances or attentions were unacceptable and unwanted.

Why?

Well, for starters, she was an heiress from an old, WASPy Main Line family while he was from a lower-middle-class Puerto Rican family. They were an unsuitable match. How could he feel comfortable on golf courses and tennis courts, at country club cocktail parties and art museum galas? He'd be way out of his comfort zone, wouldn't he? And wouldn't she be a laughingstock? A cliché? An older woman who fell for her much younger assistant. What fodder for her country club friends. The gossip would be gruesome.

Then again, Alice wasn't a stranger to gossip—when she'd quit her father's company and started her own, she was the topic of gossip for months. *I can handle that*, she thought shrewdly, but her eyes narrowed at the thought of anyone taking a shot at Carlos. She wouldn't allow it. She wouldn't subject him to it. It would destroy his credibility as a businessman in Philadelphia to be seen as her "boy toy." When it was over between them, she'd still be a Story with her own company, whereas he'd be a punchline.

Which brought her quickly to reason number two: she was thirty-three years old to his twenty-six. No matter how mature he was, seven years was an extreme difference in Alice's eyes, and she was uncomfortable with it. He was in third grade when she got her driver's license. She was graduating college when he was still in high school. It was a significant spread.

Not to mention, she felt the *loud* ticktock of her biological clock inside. She was running out of time to start a family. She had read the "thirty-five at thirty-five" research and knew that once she passed age thirty-five, her chances of getting pregnant naturally over the course of a year dipped to 35 percent, not to mention the chance of miscarriage raised to 20 percent and the chance of gestational diabetes would be at a whopping 50 percent.

No, she couldn't wait.

Once she decided on whom she wanted—and, frankly, a man like Ramirez would be a smart choice—she wanted a honeymoon baby, and one more to follow quickly after so she was finished by thirty-five. And because Alice had no intention of giving up her company or her job, her husband needed to be a man who could and would support them having a full-time nanny to look after the children, or someone who wanted to stay home and look after them himself.

This plan was problematic with Carlos for several reasons.

The first? She didn't know any twenty-six-year-old men who wanted kids. Most of them were still sowing their wild oats: dating, screwing, and having fun. Kids came later, when a man was older and settled in his mid- to late thirties.

The second? Carlos hadn't been raised like Alice. How would he feel about her going back to work after giving birth? She didn't know for certain, but she imagined that Carlos might be a little more old-fashioned when it came to children and expect his partner to stay home and raise them. Her trust would kick in after a year of marriage, so money would never be a problem, and Alice intended to love her children dearly, but subjugating her entire career to raise kids? Absolutely not. It wasn't happening.

If men could be breadwinners, leaving the rearing of children to their partners, Alice didn't see why the same couldn't be true for women.

Her feet hit the pavement hard as she panted, the rising

sun scorching her back as she segued to reason number three, the *coup de grace*: she was his boss.

And dating an employee crossed every ethical line she knew of.

She'd taken the same *workplace ethics* course at Wharton as every other MBA student, and she knew the facts: when a person in a position of greater power in a professional environment becomes romantically involved with an employee, it is never, ever a private matter or a stabilizing influence. It's disruptive to other employees, prompting questions about fairness, favoritism, transparency, credibility, and accountability. It subjected the company to an HR miasma and possible legal nightmares.

Alice's company was a well-oiled machine, thanks, in great part, to Carlos' role as office manager. But that cohesion would be destroyed when other employees caught on to their liaison. What they had worked so hard together to build would be taken down by their irresponsibility.

There were no circumstances on earth under which she would let that happen.

What was the alternative?

There was only one. If they truly intended to pursue a romantic relationship, one of them needed to find a new job so that business and personal matters could remain separate.

But *she* certainly wasn't going anywhere—it was *her* company.

And asking Carlos to find another position after the loyalty and trust he'd shown her was absolutely unthinkable. Not to mention, he was one of her greatest assets, and she worried about how smoothly her company would run without him.

He had insisted last night that it was possible for them to find a solution, but Alice vehemently disagreed. The only solution, she decided as she came to the end of the path, panting as she leaned over and rested her palms on her knees, was for them *not* to start something that had no future. So now she needed to let him know—in no uncertain terms—that a romantic relationship between them was one hundred percent out of the question. It had only taken two miles—and fifteen minutes—to make her decision.

And easy decisions were usually right.

Except, as she straightened up and looked at the bright-blue water, sparkling with sunlight that kissed wave peaks like diamonds, her eyes filled with tears that blurred the pretty scene.

Her body wanted him.

Her heart wanted him.

Some strong and deep part of Alice Story already loved Carlos Vega, and now that she'd recognized that love, forcing herself to turn her back on those feelings—while still seeing him every day—would be agony.

Reaching up to swipe at her eyes, she started running slowly back down the path toward her room, her steps as heavy as her aching heart.

***

Carlos had hit the gym a little after five, hoping to see Alice on the treadmill—he'd heard the sound of her hotel room door opening and closing ten minutes before, and he knew she was going for an early-morning run. But she wasn't there, and his heart had dropped with disappointment as he proceeded with his own workout.

It was an angry workout.

A frustrated workout.

He thought back on last night, on the feeling of Alice in his arms as they danced to that sweet, sentimental song under the stars. The way it felt for her fingers to curl into his shirt and caress the skin on the back of his neck. She was delicate but strong, and after knowing what it felt like to hold her, not clueing her into his feelings would have been like lying.

It hadn't gone well, he thought, staring at himself in the mirror as he did fifty curls with thirty-pound dumbbells, beads of sweat running down his hairline and dripping onto his white T-shirt.

She'd essentially told him that there was absolutely, positively no future for them, and yet he could have sworn that she was just as attracted to him as he was to her. They certainly respected and cared deeply about each other, even though most of those emotions had been developed in an office environment. Why—in her mind—was the jump from attraction, respect, and caring to love so impossible? Because for him, it had happened a long time ago.

Dropping the weights onto the rack, he jumped back on the cross-trainer and set it for a punishing pace.

He truly didn't care if they were from different worlds, because he meant what he'd said last night: for the past three years, they'd shared the same one. And they were so fucking good at sharing it, it made him crazy that she wouldn't even consider sharing more.

And her age?

Fuck her age. Seven years was nothing to him. His parents were ten years apart.

Besides, he was sick of girls his age, girls like Alicia-Felicia-Leticia. He was sick of one-night stands and playing the field. He'd fucked many, and it had been fun. But now he wanted more. When he thought about his cousin Diego, who had a new baby girl, or his older sister, who was pregnant with her second baby, Carlos felt a surge of longing to start a family of his own. But he wanted that family with the woman he loved.

And for better or worse, he loved his boss.

He loved Alice Story.

Panting from exertion, he pressed the stop button on the machine and stepped off, appreciating the burn in his legs. Better than the god-awful burn in his stupid fucking heart.

He grabbed a towel from the basket by the door and swung open the door of the gym, stopping in his tracks when he saw Alice, dressed in next to nothing and as sweaty as him, holding onto the chain-link fence of the tennis court on his right as she stretched her legs.

Mierda.

He took a deep breath and dried his face, heading over to talk to her. They still had five more days on this trip. Leaving things as they had last night wouldn't be comfortable for either of them.

"Alice!" he called as he approached her, watching as she froze at the sound of her name. She was bending at the waist to touch her toes, but after a second, she rolled her body up to face him.

And *oh, mami.* His fantasies? The ones about what Alice wore while she worked out? Requited. She wore a black-and-magenta sports bra with high-waisted black Lycra shorts that showed a strip of her toned stomach. And fuck, she looked just as good as he knew she would. Firm muscles, white skin, and small curves he ached to touch. His heart skipped a beat, and his mouth watered.

"Morning," she said, her voice tight. Tense.

"Morning," he said, scrubbing the towel over his short, bristly hair. "Sleep okay?"

He could see on her face that she hadn't, but she

nodded. "Just fine. You?"

"Fine."

"You know," she said, "it's good we ran into each other before today's meetings. I need to speak to you." She gestured to the path that led back to their rooms. "Walk with me?"

He knew her tone. It was the one she used when she fired someone or when she told a business partner that she didn't intend to renew a contract. She had bad news, and it had everything to do with him.

"Sure," he said, sounding cool even though his insides were in a knot.

They set out at a leisurely pace, but he noted that she made sure there was enough space between them that their arms didn't brush together.

"Carlos, you're a very valued employee at Story Sisters. I don't know how I would have started my own company without you. I will always be grateful for your trust and loyalty." She paused, clearing her throat. "And neither of us could have foreseen that something as seemingly innocent as a dance would have led to the disclosure of inappropriate feelings, but unfortunately, it did."

Or fortunately, he thought, *because I'm not sorry you know how I feel.*

"I regret letting my emotions get the better of me and leaving you alone at the table. I hope you'll forgive that rudeness on my part."

"Alice—"

"But that doesn't change the fact that what happened between us cannot happen again. In fact, I shouldn't have indulged the conversation for as long as I did. The moment you admitted flirting with me, I should have cut it off at the knees. I apologize for engaging in any dialogue that might have led you to believe that there is any chance for a romantic relationship between us. Because there isn't."

He clenched his hands into fists of frustration by his sides. "You're making a mistake."

"No," she said evenly. "I'm doing what's right."

"This is complicated," he said. "And I get that, Allie, but—"

"This conversation is over," she said, "and if you bring it up again, I'll assume that your position at Story Sisters isn't important enough to—"

"You're *threatening* me?" he cried, reaching for her arm and spinning her around to face him. He searched her eyes, finding them rolling with emotion. "Are you *that scared* of what's going on between us?"

She flinched, her chest heaving as she inhaled a sharp breath and held it for several seconds before releasing it. "Let go of my arm."

He uncurled his fingers. "Fine. Whatever you say, boss."

Shaking his head with disappointment—in both her and the situation—he turned away from her, walking on his own back to his room and ignoring her as she called out to him.

He opened his door and slammed it shut, punching the tiled wall in his room, which bloodied one of his knuckles.

"Fuck this," he hissed, throwing the gym towel to the floor, then whipping his shirt over his head and his underwear and workout shorts down his legs.

Entering the bathroom, he turned on the hot water and stepped into the shower, searching his mind for a past conversation with Alice that would give him context for this one. But he came up frustratingly blank. He'd been in hundreds of meetings with Alice and listened to her on a thousand different phone calls, but he'd never seen her back away from a situation because it scared her. Not with her father. Not with her sisters. Not with her banker or her employees or investors or the guy at customs who occasionally held one of their shipments for longer than necessary. Alice didn't retreat from battle or conflict; she mastered it and made it her bitch.

But the idea of being with him?

It had shut her down in a way he'd never witnessed before. She didn't know what to do with her feelings for him and his for her. So for the first time that he could remember, she was running away.

That's how affected she is by this, he thought. *By you. By the idea of us.*

It was the only thought that calmed his racing blood and made him close his eyes in surrender to the hot water sluicing over his aching, tired body.

Alice was in the deep end of the ocean right now, and he wasn't sure she knew how to swim. But a man in love doesn't leave his woman to the sharks. No. He swims out, puts his arms around her, and pulls her safely back to shore even if she insists that she's "fine."

Opening his eyes, he ran his soapy hands through his hair.

Then again, sharks have their uses, he thought, letting his lips quirk up in a tiny grin as he narrowed his eyes and planned his next move. *Yes, indeed. Sharks could* sometimes *be useful.*

***

"You see, Miss Story…" continued Francisco Galletín, the head vintner at *Bahía de Plata*, launching into another thirty-minute explanation about the soil and climate.

Alice nodded politely as he glanced up at her from where he knelt in the dirt, but she was having trouble concentrating. They'd toured the wine-making operations all morning, stopped for a quick bite, and then continued in the vineyards for most of the afternoon. At this point, she was covered in sweat and dust, which itched like crazy. And whatever sun block she'd rubbed on before breakfast had been sweated off hours ago. When she occasionally scratched herself, her skin burned from the irritants and sunburn, and all she really wanted was to get in a cool shower and stay there for hours.

A throaty laugh distracted Alice from Mr. Galletín's discourse, and she turned around to see his assistant, Ana María, place her hand on Carlos' bare arm as she threw back her head with mirth. They had stayed behind at the winery to "inspect" the bottling process together at Ana María's suggestion. But the only inspecting going on was of Carlos' bicep by Ana María's hand.

Since they'd been introduced this morning just after breakfast, Carlos and Ana María had been inseparable, walking at the back of the group, chuckling together, and speaking in rapid Spanish.

Alice's stomach flipped over for the tenth or twentieth time, but she whipped her head around before Carlos could notice her pique. Especially after the disgraceful ending to her lecture this morning, at which point she'd embarrassed both of them by resorting to idle threats, she had no right to him and no right to feel jealous of another woman's attentions toward him—no matter how much they were bothering her.

"When we first contracted the grapes from Spain…" Mr. Galletín continued, leading Alice farther away from the shade of the winery and deeper into the hot, dusty vineyard rows. Her high heels were ill-suited to the dirt, but she did her best to keep up and appear interested.

Carlos certainly wasn't having trouble appearing interested.

Not at all.

In fact, Ana María had to be the most fascinating creature on the face of the entire fucking earth, the way Carlos held on her every word, letting her practically maul him in public. It was none of Alice's business if they wanted to get to know one another better (a thought that made bile rise up in her throat), but they could at least be a little more discreet about it, couldn't they?

Yet another laugh floated out from the winery porch to Alice's ears, and she flinched.

Glancing over her shoulder at them—*damn it!*—her eyes slammed into Carlos'. He blinked at her, and his lips quirked into a small grin before he turned back to Ana María and said something in Spanish that had her reaching for him again, this time to flatten her hand on his chest in the exact place where Alice's hand had been last night during their dance.

"Oh!" she blurted out, jerking her gaze away from the happy pair to find Mr. Galletín's surprised face looking at her.

"Yes? Miss Story? Did you have a question about the seed maturation process?"

She took a deep breath, just about at the end of her proverbial rope.

"Señor," she said, "this is all so very fascinating, but I'm feeling a little overheated. Might we…"

"*Ay, sí,*" he said, gesturing back to the winery. "Yes, of course. Some refreshment? I can ask Ana María to—"

"No!" she exclaimed. The thought of sitting down with Carlos and Ana María for refreshments was a little too much for Alice to bear. "I mean…I think I'd like to return to my room and freshen up before our dinner tonight."

"Ah. Of course. Yes. A good idea, Miss Story," he said, his weathered face cracking into a grin. "Our sales team will be on hand to answer all your questions at dinner."

"How lovely. Thank you for your kind welcome. And"—her head was swimming, but she gestured lamely to the vines that surrounded them—"valuable and thorough instruction about the growing process."

"But of course."

"If you'll just point me in the right direction, I can make my way back up to the resort and—"

"Ana María!" he called. "*Terminó el paseo. Quizás puedas llevar a Miss Story a su habitación?*"

"*Con placer*," said Ana María, who turned away from Carlos and approached them. She was beautiful, young, and fit and wore a black short-sleeved T-shirt; high-cut, cuffed khaki shorts; and sensible hiking boots, which did nothing to make her long legs look less feminine and everything to make her look sensible and cool.

Carlos, walking behind her, locked his gaze with Alice for a moment, then dropped his eyes to Ana María's ass before looking up at his boss again.

"No!" said Alice, her heart in knots, dust and sweat making her eyes water. "Not necessary, Ana María. I can find my own way back."

"I'll take you back," said Carlos, the sound of his deep, familiar voice hurting her.

"I don't need your help," she said, but her throat was so dry, her voice broke on the word help.

Ignoring her, he turned back to their hosts. "*Gracias, Francisco y Ana. Nos vemos más tarde a la cena?*"

Ana María nodded with a winsome smile, saying something to him in Spanish before turning back toward the winery with her boss.

Alice's insides rolled with fury, confusion, and, more than anything, white-hot jealousy, such that she had never known.

Turning away from their hosts, she spoke only loud enough for Carlos to hear: "Don't deprive Ana María of your company. I can find my own way back."

"I'll see her later at dinner," he said calmly. "I don't mind walking you back."

She reached up to push a burning bead of sweat from her forehead. "Don't do me any favors."

"I'm not. I'm doing my job."

"Was it your job to flirt with the vintner's assistant nonstop all day?" she spat.

"Hey! Why are you angry with me?" he asked, taking her arm as she tried to walk over a rock cropping in heels.

She snatched her arm away, embarrassing tears blurring her vision. "Leave me alone."

"God damn it, Allie," sighed Carlos, taking her arm again. "You're going to twist your ankle."

"I'm *not* your responsibility," she choked out, leaning on him as she stepped carefully over the rocks and back onto the dirt road that led up the hill to the resort. She pulled away from him again, brushing a hateful tear from her sunburned cheek as she started walking at a brisk pace. "I'm fine now. Go back to your—your—Ana María!"

"What do you want from me, *mujer*?" he shouted at her back. "*You're* not into me, so what does it matter who I talk to?"

More frustrating tears brightened her eyes as he confessed this, but she didn't care. She was tired and sunburned and covered in sweat and dust and grime. But the thing that hurt most of all was that she wasn't strong enough to let go of him, no matter how much she needed to, and he seemed to have no problem moving on quickly from her.

Had jealousy not reared its ugly, green-eyed head, all would have been fine. Maybe over time, they could have even found their equilibrium again. But now she knew: it was too late for that.

Her feelings—inconvenient and unwanted though they were—were here to stay.

"*You* are a horse's ass!" she cried, whipping around to face him. "I *am* into you, can't you see that?"

Chapter 9

Alice's passionate words stunned Carlos into silence—he wasn't entirely sure what he should do, though they soothed a pain inside of him that had been throbbing uncomfortably all day.

"I *can't* be into you," she sobbed. She was staring down at her dirty, poorly-chosen shoes, and he couldn't tell if she was speaking to him or to herself. "This wasn't supposed to happen. I *shouldn't* be into you."

Alice and her goddamned shoulds and shouldn'ts.

Man, but he was getting sick of them.

He sighed, looking at her dusty, bright-red, miserable face and found he couldn't bear her unhappiness. Apparently a shark, in the form of the delightful and very *married* Ana María, had worked a little *too* well in raising Alice's ire. In fairness, he probably shouldn't have checked out her ass for Alice's sole benefit. Maybe that was taking it a little too far. He decided to come clean.

"I'm not into Ana María," he said softly. "Aside from the fact that I don't *know* her, she's married."

"Someone should tell her husband," she Alice, her eyes flashing. "She was all over you like a cheap suit."

"No, Allie, she wasn't inappropriate. I think it's a cultural difference," said Carlos gently. "We're more...touchy-feely here in the Caribbean. It doesn't mean anything. Ana María and I attended the same university in Puerto Rico and were trading stories. That's all."

"It didn't look like *all*," she said, crossing her arms over her chest.

"I want *you*...and you want *me*," he said fiercely, reaching for her. He put his arms around her waist, relieved when she allowed him to pull her closer. "You can fight it as hard as you want, *mi amor*, but you won't win. You'll just make us both more miserable."

She was stiff in his arms, but she also wasn't fighting him, so he didn't let her go.

"*Calmate, Allie*," he murmured, stroking her hair as her body slowly relaxed from rigid to resigned. Finally, she leaned against him, her cheek falling to his chest with a weary sigh. "*Está bien, mi amor. Te lo prometo. Estará bien.*"

"*Bien* means good. But this is *not* good, Carlos. It's not good at all," she said softly, her voice heavy and grieved.

"You don't know that," he argued, keeping his voice gentle but firm. "We won't know that unless we talk about it. Unless we try to figure it out."

"You could have anyone," she said, changing tactics. "Women throw themselves at you. Maybe not Ana María, but the waitress last night. Every woman in our office—"

"So what? It doesn't matter."

"It matters to me." Her voice was small when she continued. "And you encourage it. You checked out her ass."

He chuckled softly at her jealousy. "Want to know something?"

"I don't know."

"Alice…I wasn't checking out her ass. I was only trying to make you a little jealous. I needed your jealousy to tell me whether or not you were telling the truth this morning."

"I was."

Her words pierced his heart like a dagger.

"*What?*" he asked, leaning back to look at her face.

"I *was* telling the truth. We should…stop this before it begins. It would be best for both of us."

"Only if we have no feelings for each other," he said, searching her eyes. "Tell me that you don't care for me and I will let you go right now."

She'd been holding her breath, but she released it slowly, turning away from him with a quiet sob as she rested her cheek back on his chest. Her silence was his answer, and his shoulders slumped in relief, his heart filling with gladness.

He pressed his lips to her hair and held her tight. "I'm not interested in anyone but you, *mi amor*. And from now on, you'll never doubt it. I promise. I only have eyes for you…and *your* ass."

"Carlos!"

"It's true," he said, smiling as he kissed her hair again. "I want *you*. I keep telling you this. At some point, you'll have to trust me."

"I *do*," she said, her eyes shiny and wide as she leaned back to gaze up at him. "I *do* trust you. I trust you more than any other man on earth, Carlos."

He suspected as much, but he knew from the husky tone of her voice and the look in her eyes that she was telling him an important and sacred truth.

"Then trust me when I say we can figure this out together."

He reached for her cheek and cupped it in his palm, tempted to kiss her for the first time, but she flinched in pain, and he lifted his hand to look at the angry burn underneath.

"You're burned," he noted with a grimace.

"It hurts like hell," she said.

"You need to wear better sun block tomorrow," he said, dropping his hand to clasp hers and leading her up the dirt road back toward the resort.

He wasn't going to force a first kiss on someone who was grimy, achy, and uncomfortable. He wanted it to be as good as he'd dreamed; as perfect as he knew it could be. Not to mention, knowing Alice, it would be better to wait until they had talked tomorrow; he didn't want to move too fast and jeopardize the fragile possibilities between them.

"Do you have aloe for the burn?"

She shook her head. "I didn't realize how strong the sun would be."

"I'll get you some. You go to your room and I'll grab some lotion at the shop in the lobby and bring it to you."

"You're good to me," she said, her hand still entwined in his, a little miracle that he welcomed.

"I take care of you. That's what I do, *querida*. That's what I've done for three years. And that's *all* I want to do for the rest of—"

She gasped softly, and he bit his lip, swallowing back the words. It was too soon for them.

"—the trip."

"Oh," she sighed and nodded, her relief palpable.

They walked in silence for several minutes, their feet crunching against the dirt and pebbles until they reached the paved path around the perimeter of the resort where Alice had taken her morning run. He hated to drop her hand, but more, he couldn't stand for her to be in discomfort if there was anything he could to do make it better.

"Go take a cool shower. I'll leave the lotion outside your door, okay?"

She nodded, taking a step away from him before looking up at him with such confusion, it made his heart clench. "What about...everything else?"

He leaned forward to push a flyaway strand of her blonde hair behind her ear. "Our flight to Ponce tomorrow doesn't leave until five. We have the whole day together and no more meetings. How about we talk tomorrow?"

She gulped, and for a moment he thought she'd say no and launch into another speech about why they were impossible, but instead, she nodded. "Okay. We'll talk tomorrow."

She started walking toward her room, but he stopped her. "Allie!"

She turned to face him. "Yes?"

"Sit next to me at dinner?"

She grinned at him, a smile that came to her lips so suddenly and so easily, it almost knocked him off his feet. "*Sí. Con placer.*"

"Look at you learning Spanish!"

She shrugged, but he could tell she was happy. "Just a little bit."

Butterflies swarmed in his chest as he grinned back at her. "Now go cool off that jealousy, *querida.*"

"Cocky," she murmured, leaning down to take off her shoes before turning around and walking back to her room barefoot.

Not cocky.

Happy, he thought, watching until she was out of sight before heading up to the lobby store. His steps were lighter than they'd been all day...because no matter what she'd said to him this morning, there was still a chance for them.

And a chance was all he needed.

***

The sound of her alarm cut into another superhot dream Alice was having about Carlos, and her eyes fluttered opened to her hotel room bathed in morning sunlight.

"Ahhh," she sighed, hitting snooze. She rolled onto her back and closed her eyes, trying to savor the last few seconds of dreamy sweetness.

Last night at dinner, they'd sat beside each other as he'd requested, and for most of the dinner, he'd held her hand under the table, though Alice had been unaware of how many different—and incredibly provocative—ways there were to touch someone else's hands and fingers.

At times his grip had been light, with one of his much larger, rougher fingers running leisurely up and down one of hers. Other times, he'd lace their fingers together and make lazy circles in her palm with the pad of his thumb, distracting her from conversation with the *Bahía de Plata* investors by wondering how it would feel for his finger to be circling a very different place on her body, which was wet and slick from his touch and her imagination.

By the time they'd returned to their rooms at midnight, she'd been overstimulated, sexually frustrated, and drop-dead exhausted. When he'd pulled her to him, wrapping his arms around her, she'd licked her lips, ready to be kissed, but he'd pressed his lips to her forehead instead, then wished her, "*Buenos Noches, querida.*"

She'd leaned back and looked up at him, disappointment surely stark on her face.

He'd smiled at her knowingly, his voice almost hypnotic. "We'll talk tomorrow."

"But…"

"Believe me, *mi amor*," he'd said, holding her close

enough that she could feel the thick, long ridge of his erection pressing against her stomach, "I would kiss you all over, all night long…but I know you. We need to talk first—to put your mind at ease."

Her body cried out with want, but she'd somehow managed to nod, letting him spin her around so she faced the door to her room. With shaking fingers, she'd swiped the keycard over the reader and entered her room, knowing that she'd be back in his arms if she'd just turn around.

Last night's dreams, charged though they were, had been a poor substitute for the real thing, and Alice opened her eyes again, pouting for a second before whipping off the covers.

Exercise. Exercise would help, right?

She reached into her suitcase for a neon-yellow-and-orange sports bra and paired it with Lycra shorts that were black with a neon-yellow stripe down each side. She pulled her hair back into a high ponytail, then grabbed some socks and slipped her feet into sneakers. Tucking the keycard into her bra, she opened the door, jumping a foot when she heard someone say, "Good morning, *bonita*!"

"Ah!" she yelled, clutching at her chest and backing up against the closed door of her room.

Carlos' shoulders began shaking with laughter. "Er, um…I thought I'd join you this morning?"

"But scare me to death first?" she asked, punching him lightly on his bare arm.

He was wearing a sleeveless white T-shirt that showed off his bulging biceps and loose gray running shorts low on his hips. He was tall and strong and beautiful, and her body ached for the weight of his on top of hers.

"I waited for half an hour. Didn't want to miss you."

Sliding her eyes from his chest to his face, she grinned

at him and leaned against her door, which thrust her breasts toward him. "You did?"

His eyes dropped to her chest for a moment, and she watched his jaw flex before he nodded, letting his gaze slide back up her body and reclaim hers. "I generally work out in a gym, but I could be persuaded to change my ways."

"Why would you do that?"

He shrugged. "Because I get to spend more time with you."

She couldn't help the way her whole body responded to this simple sweetness, and she stepped forward, so close to him, they were almost touching. "Why would you want to spend *more* time with me?"

"Aside from the fact that I'm crazy about you?" He scratched his chin. "I don't know. Maybe because we should discuss whether or not you felt the vineyard operation here was a viable structure for the Ramirez land in Ponce."

"Ahhh," she sighed dramatically. "A man who can talk business."

"Fastest way to my woman's heart." He gestured toward the tennis courts with a tilt of his head. "Come on. Let's go. Tell me what you think on the way."

They walked briskly for a warm-up, their arms occasionally touching and sending chills down Alice's arm every time. She told him that she was impressed with the operation at *Bahía de Plata* and liked that local farmers had been tapped to run the day-to-day operations.

"But Señor Galletín mentioned a partnership between the Dominican Republic, the United States, Spain, and Chile, didn't he?" asked Alice.

"*Sí*, he did."

"Hmm," she hummed, thinking. "I don't believe that was something that, um, Ram—Ramirez, um…mentioned."

She stuttered on his name, suddenly remembering the flirty, forward texts they'd exchanged in the car on Thursday morning and starting to regret them. Without being lewd, Alice had essentially set the scene for romance, or at least for them to become more familiar during her visit. And Ramirez's enthusiastic replies had assured her of his interest. Interest that now seemed far from what she actually wanted. She grimaced in thought.

"Alice?"

"Huh?"

"You were saying about the partnership?"

"Oh, um...I don't believe Mr. Ramirez mentioned such a partnership."

"Is it possible he's hoping to start his operation with all private investors?" asked Carlos, pausing in front of one of the tennis courts to stretch.

Alice's heart sped up as it always did when she was lying...or hiding something. If she was upset about Carlos flirting with Ana María yesterday, certainly he'd have a right to be upset with her about Ramirez.

Her stomach flipped uncomfortably at the thought of jeopardizing whatever was happening between them. As the seconds ticked by, she knew, more and more, how hard it would be to let him go now.

"Um...I don't know."

Carlos stopped stretching and stood up, looking at her closely, his eyes narrowing. "Hey...are you okay?"

"Yes!" she said too quickly, hating the way her heart fluttered with guilt.

"Sure?"

She bent down and touched her toes so he'd stop looking at her so closely. "Uh-huh. Fine. Just...thinking."

As soon as they got to Ponce, she'd just have to let

Ramirez know, as politely as possible, that she was no longer interested in anything but business. Nothing had actually happened yet, right? Just the exchange of some flirty texts. Stop worrying…

"So I had an idea," said Carlos.

Alice stood up straight, looking at him. "What?"

"We race."

"Race? Oh, I don't usually—"

"Excellent. It's decided. We race. And if I win, you kiss me. And if you win, you kiss me. Deal?" His lips wobbled, and he grinned at her. "Onyourmarkgetsetgo!"

Before she could agree to his ridiculous terms, he was off like a shot, running down the paved path in front of her, and with a giggle of anticipation, her worrisome thoughts scattered, and she started after him.

***

Carlos hadn't planned to ask for a kiss already—today had barely begun, after all. But the way she looked? In that tight outfit over her hot body? *Mierda*. He was lost. He could barely concentrate on their conversation about the vineyards, and she seemed just as distracted as him.

Fuck, he wanted her.

Bad.

Listening to her chuckle from behind him, he smiled, puffing through his exertion, appreciating the wind in his hair as a breeze rolled off the ocean. Was it possible it could be this simple? That he could insist that they could figure it out, and voilà, they would? Because after three years of silently wanting Alice, it felt almost too easy. Not that he valued his prize any less, but he worried a little that the road to true love couldn't possibly be this smooth.

Like a little bullet, she surged in front of him on the path, and he almost tripped and fell, her trim hips and tight ass on full display as she pulled ahead.

Damn, but my woman's got some fine curves, he thought, speeding up to be closer to her.

She looked at him over her shoulder, toying with him, slowing her pace just a touch, then surging forward again when he was only an arm's length away.

Despite the burning of his lungs, he laughed softly to himself, enjoying this new side of his boss—playful and fun. It foreshadowed how she'd be in bed, he thought, his body tightening at the thought.

She turned back, her voice barely breathless as she called, "Come on! Who's the younger one here?"

Because Carlos engaged in strength training more than cardio, she was kicking his ass, but he was going to add a lot more cardio to his schedule. This was the last time he'd let her beat him in a run.

"Obviously you!" he shouted back, and her laughter floated on the breeze to him, unusual and lyrical, making him smile in spite of himself.

It also gave him a good opening to for discussing their disparity in age, something that obviously bothered her. He sped up a little, and she slowed down as he approached, shooting him a grin. "You holding up okay?"

"Yeah," he answered, wiping the sweat off his upper lip. "You're a machine."

She glanced at him. "I stay in shape."

"For the record? Your ass beats Ana María's any day and twice on Sunday."

"Is that right?"

"That is one hundred percent a fact, *mami*."

"*Mami?*"

"It's slang. Like, sarcastic, truth-slang."

"So you're not really calling me 'mommy.'"

"Alice, when I call you 'baby' later, it won't have nothin' to do with seein' you as a child either."

"Are you going to call me 'baby'?" she asked.

He nodded. "Hell yes."

"When would that be?"

"When you're lyin' beneath me...*baby*."

Her neck jerked, and she faced him with wide eyes. "Whoa. You just went there."

"I *been* there, *mami*. Just waitin' for you to come join me."

"Damn," she breathed, speeding up and pulling away from him.

Nope. Not happening. He dug deep and gained on her.

"Stop runnin' away from me."

"I'm not running away from you. I'm in a rush to win or lose," she said all sassy, speeding up yet again.

He didn't try to catch up with her this time, just watched the beauty of her body in motion as she ran down the straight path and reached the end. When she stopped, he stopped too, still about thirty yards from her, and started walking. She panted, her hands on her hips, her eyes dark as they held his.

As he approached her, his steps sped up, and suddenly he was running toward her, and she was running toward him, her eyes dropping to his lips when they were inches away.

He reached for her hips, lifting her against his body and holding her with one arm as their mouths collided, hungry and insistent, his other hand clasping the back of her neck to hold her close. Her hands landed on the back of his skull, a deep moan releasing from her throat. He swallowed it hungrily, parting her lips with his tongue, tasting the salt of her sweat and the sea air, exploring the sweet recesses of her mouth, still minty from brushing her teeth. She arched her back, and he leaned forward so her feet could touch the ground as his tongue slid against hers, learning the softness of this goddess who'd been elusive for so long. He slid his hand down her back, over her damp, sun-warmed skin, over the Lycra of her bra, and rested it on the skin between her bra and shorts, needing to feel her, to touch her, to know that this was—*finallyfinallyfinally*—real.

He leaned back for a moment, staring down at her closed eyes, which opened slowly.

"This is happening, baby," he whispered.

"Apparently."

"It's gonna keep happening, Allie," he whispered, breathless with desire and need.

"Good," she said, pulling his head back down to hers. "More."

"Day-umn," he groaned, grinning at her as he dropped his lips to hers once again.

Their second kiss was less frantic, and he sank into it, tightening his arms around her smaller body and reveling in the touch of her warm skin. Her hands laced around the back of his neck, her forearms resting on his shoulders, her sweet, soft lips moving against his, her tongue slow dancing with his. And even where clothing separated them, he could still feel the rigid points of her nipples pressed against his chest and knew that she could feel his rock-hard erection cradled between her thighs.

I love you, he thought. *I love you, you driven, smart, beautiful, sexy woman. I love you like crazy. I have for the longest time.*

A loud, whistled catcall made them pull apart, cheek to cheek and panting as they turned toward the beach to find a group of three teenage boys taunting them from the sand.

"Yeah, man! Give it to her!"

"Grab her ass for me, man!"

"Get a room, yo!"

Carlos stiffened at their lewd remarks about Alice, but he was stopped from pounding them into politeness by the feeling of Alice's chest trembling again his. He turned to look at her face, finding it radiant in a full-blown smile and laughter she could barely contain.

"Point taken," she called, waving at the boys. "Thanks for caring!"

"I am happy to beat them up for you," said Carlos, looking down into her eyes.

"Not necessary."

"More kissing?" he asked hopefully.

"Not here and not now."

"Then let's go somewhere else?"

She nodded, letting him entwine their fingers together. "Aren't we racing back?"

"Have pity on my poor body," he said, setting the pace just short of brisk.

"Your body is seven years younger than mine."

"Okay, baby, we're gonna talk about this."

She sighed. "It's a fact. I'm older."

"It's a number. You're in better shape."

She darted a quick look at the bicep closest to her. "No chance."

"I could lift more, but you've got me beat in cardio."

"Perfect together, huh?"

He didn't allow her flirty comment to derail him. "Alice, I don't care that you're thirty-three, and here's the truth: I will never care that you're a few years older than me. My father's ten years older than my mother, and they've been happy for thirty years."

He couldn't be positive, but it felt like her fingers squeezed his.

"Really?" she asked.

"Really. Seven is nothing."

"I don't know…"

"Who does it bother?" he asked. "You?"

She shrugged. "A little."

"So much that you don't want to be with me?"

She didn't hesitate before shaking her head. "No."

"You've got to decide that it doesn't bother you, baby, because I don't wanna keep having this conversation. We're seven years apart. Can you handle it or not?"

"You were nine when I was sixteen."

"Yeah. And I'll be seventy-one when you're seventy-eight."

She scoffed softly beside him. "Think we'll still know each other then?"

Yes.

"No one knows what the future holds, but I hope so."

This time he wasn't uncertain—her fingers squeezed his. He lifted them to his lips and kissed her knuckles. "I don't care about numbers. I'm *loco* for you, *mi amor.*"

"I know what that means," she said, her voice full of warmth and happiness. "I'm crazy about you too."

"So you'll stop worrying? About our ages?"

She nodded. "I'll try."

For several minutes, they walked in comfortable silence, letting new truths settle between them as they held hands, the warm ocean breeze and rising sun bathing their faces.

"What else is bothering you?" he asked as the tennis courts came into view.

"Lots," she said, her voice dipping from sunny to heavy as she glanced up at him.

"Tell me."

"If I think about returning to the office, I might have a

panic attack."

"So let's not tackle that one right now. But what else? There's more. I can feel it." When she didn't respond, he thought about what she'd said on Thursday night after their dance: *We're from different worlds.*

"Would you be…"

He cleared his throat, hating the question he was about to ask, mostly because he feared her answer. Alice wasn't a shallow person, but still…

"Would I be…what?" she asked.

"I'm from Puerto Rico. I don't have an MBA. I'm less successful than you. Hell, I'm your *assistant*. Would you be *embarrassed* to—?"

She stopped walking, tugging her hand from his. Her eyes were angry and her lips tight as she stared up at him. "To what?"

"To introduce me as your…boyfriend?"

"You listen to me," she said, her eyes brightening as she poked him in the chest with one finger, "I don't give a *shit* what anyone says about me. I grew a Teflon shell years ago. It comes with the territory."

Instinctively, he knew she was referring not just to her social position in Philadelphia but to being her father's daughter.

"So," he said, plucking her finger from his chest and kissing the tip, "that's a no to embarrassment?"

"That's a no to embarrassment," she whispered. "Except…"

"What?"

"*You.* It's possible…I mean…You'll be a joke for a while," she said, lifting her chin and gulping softly. "My much younger boyfriend. My assistant. Hot and young and…" Her voice broke off, and she turned away from him.

Now he understood.

She wasn't concerned with people talking about her. She was worried about him looking a fool. And God, that was so like her, it made his heart clench with love for her. She didn't care what anyone said about her…but she cared that his reputation might take a hit.

"Baby," he whispered, putting his hands on her shoulders and turning her around, "you think *I* give a shit what the country club set thinks of me?"

"I don't know. Do you?" she asked, her wide eyes scanning his face.

"I care about one thing," he said, cupping her sweet face. "*You.*" He leaned down and pressed his lips to hers. A sweet kiss, lingering just long enough to steal his breath and foreshadow what he wanted to do to her whole body as soon as they were alone together. "Everyone else can go fuck themselves."

She blinked up at him, the muscles in her face relaxing. "Really?"

"Really, *mi amor*," he said, still cradling her cheek in his hand as a rain cloud covered the sun. "I walked away from your father's company because I believed *in you*. I didn't care about anything—or anyone—else, and so far, that choice was the best decision I ever made. In my whole life."

Her eyes closed, and she turned her face into his hand, her lips pressing against his palm, her tongue darting out to lick his warm skin, making his cock twitch with need.

"Take me back to my room," she murmured, her lips caressing his hand as she formed the words in a whisper. She opened her eyes and looked up at him, her voice deep with need as raindrops began dotting her beautiful face. "Take me to bed, Carlos."

"Are you sure, Allie? Once we cross that line, I'm not

stepping back. You'll be mine, *mi amor*. And once you belong to me, I don't intend to walk away. Ever."

"I know." She nodded, pulling his hand from her face to kiss his knuckles. Then she lowered their hands between them, still holding his tightly as rainwater sluiced down his arm. "I'm sure. I'm yours."

Chapter 10

Alice swiped her card over the reader and opened the door, holding it for him to follow her inside, then leaned against it as he stood several feet away with his back to her and his hands on his hips. The only things she could hear were the pitter-patter of rain outside, the thunder of her heartbeat in her ears, and the lightning-quick panting of her breath.

Without turning around, Carlos toed off his sneakers, first the left, then the right. Resting the back of her head against the hotel room door and unable to look away, she traced the movement of his arms as he dropped his fingers to the edge of his T-shirt. Slowly, so that every muscle on his beautiful back rippled in slow, controlled waves, he raised the white cotton over his head and threw it to the floor.

Blisteringly aware of what was about to happen between them, she stared at the smooth, caramel-color skin of his back, balling her hands into fists at her sides as her lower lip slipped between her teeth.

Pivoting on one socked foot, he turned around and approached her, his careful, deliberate movements lionlike, stalking her from where she stood. Without dropping her eyes for a moment, he reached for her hands and unfurled her fingers, then pinned her arms over her head, holding her wrists against the door with one hand while the other landed on her waist.

"Fast or slow?" he asked, dropping his lips to the exposed skin just over her sports bra.

"Both," she panted.

"Good answer," he said, dragging his lips over her flesh, his tongue darting out to lick drops of rain.

"Hard or soft?" he asked, reaching for the zipper between her breasts and pulling it down slowly, the sound of each tooth it opened echoing in the chaos of her mind.

"Both," she answered breathlessly.

"*Sí, mi amor,*" he said as the zipper cleared the bottom and he separated the sides, baring her naked breasts to him, "both."

Bending his head, he nuzzled the valley between her breasts, cradling the left in the palm of his hand as he licked the nipple of her right with one long, broad-tongued stroke.

She whimpered, bowing her back, fighting lightly against the way her wrists were pinned over her head but stopping when his grip tightened.

His lips latched onto the throbbing bud he'd just licked, and he sucked strongly as his thumb massaged its twin. Alice moaned loudly, arching into his mouth as his tongue laved the sensitive skin. He slid is lips between the swells of flesh and tongued her other nipple in slow, wet circles. Taking the rigid skin between his lips, he suckled on her flesh, making her already damp panties flood with moisture. She cried out, the sound animalistic and sharp, a combination of satiety and hunger.

Releasing her nipple with a kissing noise, Carlos lifted his head to look up at her, loosening his grip on her wrists and lowering her arms.

"Allie?"

She was breathless and dizzy as her bra slipped down her arms and fell to the floor. "Mm?"

"I'm takin' you to bed."

"Mm-hm," she said, ready to follow him around the world if he told her that's where they were going.

Holding one of her hands, he led her over to the bed and sat down on the edge, reaching for her hips. Staring deeply into her eyes, he hooked his fingers into the waistband of her shorts and panties and yanked. He took the hand he was holding and put in on his shoulder, then leaned forward and guided her clothing down to her ankles.

The tight black coils of his hair rested against the brown curly hair over her clit, and she felt her body flush at the incredibly erotic image of his face so close to her sex.

"Hold on to me," he growled, and she curled her fingers onto his shoulder.

Picking up one of her feet, he unlaced her sneaker, then slipped her shoe, sock, and half of her shorts off. He picked up the other foot and did the same, throwing her shorts and panties well out of reaching distance and leaving her naked before him.

Lifting his head slowly, she felt the light pressure of his skull sliding upward, his hair tickling her belly as wide, dark eyes looked up at her. One hand slipped behind her and rested flat on her ass as he pushed her closer to him. The other flattened over her clit, the heel if his hand pressing insistently against her.

"You're soaked for me."

Alice's previous lovers had never spoken in such graphic, erotic terms, and her breath caught as she looked down at him, unable to speak, only nodding slightly as her cheeks flared with heat.

"I'm dying to taste you, Allie."

Her mouth dropped open, and she nodded again.

His lips quirked up, and he licked them. "I wasn't asking for permission, baby. You're mine. Remember?"

She bit her bottom lip, a rare feeling of vulnerability changing the nature of her persona. She was no longer a business owner with the weight of the world on her shoulders; she was a woman. Hot blooded and aching. Just a woman who was desperately in love with a man who made her feel hot and needy, safe and desired, protected and wanted. Her smile answered his as she stepped closer to him, between his outstretched legs where his erection tented the flimsy material of his running shorts.

"You're the boss at the office, Allie. But here?" He stood up, then reached for her hips, turning her so that they traded places and the backs of her knees touched the bed. "I'm in charge."

She could barely breathe, his words so commanding, so certain, she couldn't do anything but nod again.

"Understand?" he asked.

"Yes," she murmured, her clit throbbing for his promised touch.

"Lie down."

She sat down on the bed, holding his eyes as she edged back on her elbows.

"All the way back."

She reached back with her hands, then slid her body back and laid her head on the pillows at the head of the bed.

"Bend your knees, baby."

She bent them.

"Now spread them."

She gulped, widening the space between her legs as she heard the sound of him shucking off his shorts and dropping them to the tiled floor. His weight depressed the bed as he knelt down on the mattress.

"Close your eyes, *mi amor*."

Slowly she closed them, giving over the last of any control to him as she felt the warmth of his hot breath against her skin. With her eyes closed, every touch was heightened, and when his lips dropped to the inside of her thigh, she whimpered.

"Allie…Allie…Allie…" he groaned, spreading the lips of her sex and bathing her with his tongue—one long, slow lick from the opening of her sex to the hood of her clit.

"Oh, my God," she moaned.

He pushed his hands under each cheek of her ass and held her against his mouth, teasing her by sliding his tongue into the slick grooves on either side of her throbbing bud. Alice cried out softly, holding her breath, then releasing it as he circled her clit before licking it with broad, rhythmic strokes.

Her hips tried to buck, but he held her firmly, feasting on her pulsing, trembling flesh until the buildup was so strong, every muscle was straining, coiled within an inch of exploding. Suddenly his tongue was gone.

"Wh-What? Why?" she murmured.

"Allie," he said, his voice low and taut, "open your eyes."

She opened them instantly, licking her dry lips as her eyes slammed into his.

"I love you," he said, staring so intensely into her eyes, it felt like he was gazing at the very fabric of her soul.

Then he dropped his head, his lips latched onto her clit, and she felt the touch of his teeth on the straining, vibrating nub of skin.

She screamed, her body falling into anarchy as ribbons

of perfect pleasure unfurled like tendrils of white-hot lightning from her sex to her toes, her fingertips, and every place in between. His tongue bathed her gently as she climaxed, as fireworks detonated behind her eyelids and spasms of delight made her body jerk and tremble in endless waves. Her fingers, curled into the comforter beneath her, twisted the fabric, and her toes pointed until her heels lifted from the bed.

It took several minutes for her to realize that he was resting his head on her stomach, the bristles of his black hair soft against her skin. Sliding her hands from the comforter to his head, she rested her fingers on her beloved and wept.

***

Carlos could feel her crying.

It had taken him a moment to distinguish between the last ripples of her orgasm and tears, but when he had, he hadn't forced her to speak. Instead he rolled to her side and pulled her against his chest spoon-style, her back pressed against him, his arm under her breasts holding her tightly. His erection pressed insistently into her back, pulsing with his own need, but he would wait for his own satisfaction until they had sorted out the reason for her sadness. Maybe he'd said "I love you" too soon, but he'd felt it so strongly in that moment, with the woman of his dreams trusting him implicitly, completely, without words or rules or reservations, he hadn't been able to hold the words inside.

"Are you okay, Allie?" he asked, pressing his lips to the back of her neck.

She sobbed softly, reaching up to hold the arm beneath her breasts. "I will be."

"Was it too much?"

"It was perfect," she whispered, the words breaking.

"Too soon, then, to say—"

"No!" she insisted. "Not too soon."

"I love you, *querida*. I do. I've loved you for so long now."

"Since when?"

He grinned, kissing her neck again. "Since you stood on a desk and asked an office full of idiots if they were sick of kissing your father's ass."

She giggled in his arms, then sniffled.

"You have no idea what it felt like to stand there on the floor, looking up at you. This may sound foolish, but you looked like the Statue of Liberty almost, offering every person in that office a chance for a better life. I was…astonished by you."

She scoffed. "You were the only one."

"I'd follow you to the ends of the earth, *mi amor*."

She was silent for a moment, breathing deeply, her lungs compressing and filling more rhythmically now. "You would?"

"I'd follow you into hell," he said softly, kissing her neck again.

"I love you too," she whispered, so softly he almost could have imagined it.

His eyes burned suddenly, and he closed them, understanding with perfect clarity why Alice was crying: because when you've waited years for the words, with little hope of ever hearing them, the moment when you do is…is…overwhelming.

"You do?"

She nodded, her hair tickling his nose as she sniffled again. "Completely. I don't who I am anymore—"

"—without you," they finished together.

Gently, as though he handled the most priceless treasure on God's earth, he turned her in his arms, looking into her eyes.

"Say it again," he murmured.

"I love you," she said, the words soft but certain.

"I love you too."

Her lips quivered, and she blinked at him.

"It makes you cry to hear it?" he asked tenderly, holding her body close to his with one arm wound around her waist and the other pillowed under his head.

A tear slid from her eye, over her nose, dropping with a tiny patter on the sheets between their faces. "I've heard it very little in my life. Those words."

He flinched when she said this. He couldn't help it. There was so much raw yearning yet no self-pity in her voice. It was a fact of her life. One that he intended to remedy.

"I love you," he said again. "I loved you yesterday. I love you today. I will love you tomorrow." He leaned forward and pressed his lips to hers. "I love you, Alice."

She gulped, her eyes searching his, her voice barely audible when she sobbed his name. "Carlos."

"I'm going to say it so much, it won't make you cry anymore. It'll just be a truth. Something that belongs to you like your business or your sisters. Me. I'll belong to you. And my love will belong to you."

She bowed her head, tucking it under his chin, and he held her tighter, knowing that she needed to feel safe, that she needed the strength of his body to reinforce the rawness of his feelings.

"Where do we go from here?" she finally asked.

"*Mi amor*, as long as we're together, we go wherever we want." She tipped her head up to look at him, and he kissed her, long and hard, swallowing her soft moan of satisfaction. "*Te amo. Te quiero. Quiero hacerte el amor.*"

"What does that mean?"

"I love you," he said, kissing the tip of her nose.

"I want you," he said, rolling her onto her back and spreading her legs so his fit between them.

"I want to make love to you," he said, surging forward so that his hard cock slipped between her folds and rubbed her clit.

"Ahhhh," she moaned. "I want that too."

His erection pulsed with need, and he thrust forward again. "Are you on the pill?"

"Y-Yes," she sighed, her eyes closed and her mouth open.

"Allie, look at me." She opened her eyes, but they were heavy and dazed. Fuck, but he needed to be inside her. His breath shuddered with want. "I've been careful."

"C-Careful?"

"I've never…I've never had sex without a condom," he said, his voice breathless as he slid between her slick folds again, the tip of his cock kissing her clit. "I've never wanted to. I've never been in love with anyone…except you."

Her eyes brightened. "I've never been in love with anyone except you."

Oh, Allie. His heart clenched with how lonely she must have been, how starved for love. And he was only too glad to give her all of his. It already belonged to her anyway.

"Have you been…safe, *mi amor*?"

"I always…ahhh…" Her words trailed off as she sighed. He was thrusting rhythmically between her lips now, massaging her clit with every stroke. "I always insist on a condom. Unless I'm…*with*…someone."

"You're *with* me now," he said, cradling her head in his hands as he held his weight above her.

"Mm-hm," she hummed, flexing her hips in tandem with him, her eyes half-lidded as she stared up at him, need etched on every beloved feature of her face. "I'm yours. Please, Carlos. I need you."

He pulled his hips back and lined up his cock at the opening of her sex. It was wet and hot against the top of his cock, and he groaned, his eyes rolling back in his head as he surged forward. Moving slowly—so slowly—he felt every ridge of her hidden skin, every ripple of her muscles. They pulled forward into the heaven of her sheath until he was fully embedded there.

"Aaaaah-leeeese," he groaned, leaning down to find her lips, kissing her madly as he drew back, then slid forward again, faster this time, their fit so tight, so perfect, he was having trouble going slow.

She whimpered beneath him, raising her legs and locking them around his upper thighs as he rocked into her, relentlessly, hungrily, their moans and groans colliding, her whimpers blending with his cries until she screamed his name, "Carlos!" and he thrust forward one final time, emptying himself into her body in hot, potent streams of bliss and vowing to love her forevermore.

***

Eight hours later, with a delicious aching between her thighs, Alice sat beside Carlos in the four-passenger chartered plane bound for Ponce, Puerto Rico, her fingers entwined through his as she looked out the window at the impossibly blue Caribbean below and relived every detail of their amazing afternoon together.

They'd made love so many times she'd lost count, passionately violating every surface of her hotel room: the bathroom sink where she'd braced her hands while he'd taken her from behind, the shower where he'd knelt between her legs and licked water from her pussy, the sofa in the small sitting room where she'd straddled him, the ottoman where he'd impaled her on his lap. There had been others too, because his cock had been in her mouth at least twice, the silken skin taut over the pulsing muscle, but she couldn't remember where, and it didn't matter. While it rained outside, their day together had blended into hours of hot orgasms and sweet *I love you*s and catnaps where he held her close before sliding into her once again.

It was love that had made today possible, she realized, because nothing else would have tempted her to stray from the straight and narrow path she'd been walking for so long. Love was the deepest yearning in her heart, the most profound longing of her soul, and Carlos loved her. The truth of it made her eyes burn even now, and she squeezed his fingers tighter. No matter what, she wouldn't give him up. Not now. Not ever.

But his words, his sweet, earnest words—*Mi amor, as long as we're together, we go wherever we want*—were naïve. She could deal with their age difference, especially since he had a precedent for it in his life. She could deal with their difference in background, because, as he'd so aptly noted, they had been sharing the same world for years now. If they intended to remain together, they'd need to discuss a timeline for marriage and children sooner or later, but she wasn't worried. She sensed that Carlos' willingness to settle down would translate to flexibility on starting a family.

But the still-unavoidable hurdle? Work. And firing him—making him pay the price of their love—wasn't fair.

So what were her options?

The only one that made sense was to offer Shane the position of interim CEO and take an indefinite leave of absence so that Carlos could remain on staff.

She winced as she thought about actually doing this. Alice had risked everything to start SST: her money, her reputation, her sanity. She'd given birth to that company and raised it into a profitable, formidable trading entity. The thought of walking away from it—even for the love of her life—scared and saddened her. And would she end up blaming him for having to choose? For having to give up her ambition in order to hold onto her love?

She sighed as the captain announced their descent.

"Already?" she asked Carlos, her voice raised over the loud propeller motor.

"The islands are side by side!" he shouted back, raising her hand to his lips. "I love you."

"I love you too," she mouthed, leaning forward to kiss him and vowing that she would figure out a way to keep him forever.

Chapter 11

Their plane taxied into the tiny airport, and Carlos held Alice's hand as they walked down the small set of stairs, claimed their rolling suitcases from the tarmac, and walked over to the terminal.

It had been the best day of his life so far, and despite the number of times he'd made love to Alice today, he was already starving for her again, aching to get her alone. She was a fever, this woman, and he never ever wanted to feel cool again.

That said, he wasn't sure what awaited them here in Ponce, and he certainly wasn't looking forward to renewing Ramirez's acquaintance. Taking a deep breath as Alice dropped his hand and preceded him into the airport, he reminded himself that, yes, she was his lover, but she was also his boss, and they were here to do a deal.

"Alice!" called a cultured voice from across a rope barrier. "This way! Over here!"

Carlos looked up to see Eduardo Ramirez dressed like a total and complete douche in bright-green pants with little white tennis rackets, a white polo shirt with the collar popped, and sunglasses, like he fancied himself a movie star.

Internally, Carlos rolled his eyes, but outwardly, he remained professional, taking Alice's rolling bag in his free hand so that she could greet their host.

But his hackles were raised almost immediately.

While Alice approached Ramirez with an outstretched hand, he decided to pull Alice into a totally inappropriate hug, patting her backside like it was his to touch, and kissing her cheek way too close to the lips that Carlos had loved all afternoon.

"Alice, you look…delicious," he said, still holding onto her.

Alice placed her hands on Ramirez's shoulders, pushing him away. "Thank you for meeting us."

Ramirez moved his sunglasses to his head and snapped his fingers over his shoulder, and a man in a black suit appeared at his side holding a bouquet of bright-red Hibiscuses in clear cellophane.

"For you," he said as his man offered the flowers to Alice.

Her cheeks brightened. "How kind."

Carlos clenched his jaw. "Which way to the car?"

"*Mira,*" said Ramirez, flicking his eyes disdainfully at Carlos. "You've brought your little helper."

Alice stepped back, shoulder to shoulder with Carlos, and lifted her chin. "You remember Carlos Vega, señor?"

"I remember he knows how to make an excellent cup of coffee," said Ramirez, reaching for Alice's free hand. He tucked it into his arm and started walking toward the airport exit, leaving Carlos and his man to follow behind.

"*Tu jefe es un pendejo,*" said Carlos to the man, whom he guessed was a year or two younger than he. *Your boss is an asshole.*

"*Quizás,*" answered the man with a shrug. "*Pero me paga,*

entonces no me importa." Maybe. But he pays me so I don't really care.

"*Como te llamas?*" asked Carlos as they walked through the revolving doors, a few steps back from Captain Douche and Alice. *What's your name?*

"*Pedro,*" he answered, "*y, que te quede claro, él no es mi jefe. Solamente me paga hacerle trabajos de vez en cuando.*" *To be clear, he's not my boss. He just pays me to do jobs every so often.*

Hmm, thought Carlos, *interesting. Then he's putting on airs big-time, isn't he? All to impress Alice?* He felt his blood heat up and his eyes narrow.

As they walked out onto the sidewalk, a long, black limo was waiting for them, parked in a no-parking zone. Pedro stepped forward to open the door for Ramirez and Alice as Carlos wheeled their bags to the truck. When the backseat door slammed shut, Carlos raised his head, stepped briskly over to the side, reopened it, and slid inside.

"You're welcome to sit in the front," said Ramirez, who sat across from him and way too close to Alice, with his arms around her shoulders.

"Alice, you look warm," he commented, ignoring Ramirez.

"I am a bit warm," she said, scooting over a little, out of reach of their host.

Carlos slid his eyes back to Ramirez. "*Tiene modales, señor?*" *Do you have manners, sir?*

"*Porque? Tú vas a ensenarmelos, muchacho?*" *Why? Are you going to teach them to me, kid?*

"*Si lo necesito.*" *If I need to.*

"What are you saying?" asked Alice, looking back and forth between them. "What are you telling each other?"

"I'm just reminding Mr. Ramirez, with all due respect, that we're here for business," said Carlos.

"And I'm reminding Mr. Vega, with all due respect, that

my business is with you, *bonita*, not him."

Alice shifted uncomfortably in her seat, giving Carlos a look that told him to please try to get along. He nodded curtly at her, turning to look out the tinted windows.

So…was this even Ramirez's car? Or had he rented it to impress Alice? Why? From all accounts, Ramirez was loaded. Carlos sighed. *Maybe his car was in the shop or something.*

"*En que hotel te hospedaras?*" asked Ramirez. *What hotel are you staying in?*

Carlos turned back to their host just as Alice spoke brusquely. "Please stop doing that. It's unspeakably rude. Please speak in English."

"Of course, *querida*," said Ramirez, reaching for her hand and patting it. "I apologize. I was just wondering where Mr. Vega is staying. We can drop him at his hotel on the way to my hacienda."

Alice whipped her hand from Ramirez's grasp, shooting a desperate look at Carlos. So desperate, in fact, he almost chuckled. *Don't worry, baby*, he thought. *I wouldn't make you go into the lion's den alone.*

"I understood Alice and I were staying with you, señor," he said, playing dumb. "Did I misunderstand the plan?"

Ramirez's lips tightened to an angry line, but he shook his head, anxious not to further upset Alice, who still looked annoyed. "You're welcome at my house, of course. I just— well, I was certain my assistant told me that you were staying at the Howard Johnson's."

"No," said Carlos. "I have no reservation anywhere in town."

"Then of course you must stay at *Hacienda del Mar* with me and Alice." He turned to Alice. "My son, young Ricardo, is visiting. I hope you will like meeting him."

"I'm sure I will," said Alice, her chilly expression warming just a little at the mention of Ramirez's son.

How will you be as a mother? wondered Carlos, daring, just for a moment, to imagine her stomach swollen with his child and surprised by how it stole his breath to imagine it. A baby, a little girl or boy with her blonde hair and his dark eyes. Would their child be fair like her or dark like him?

He realized he was staring at her, her smile answering the one that must have spread across his own face.

Ramirez cleared his throat loudly, and both Alice and Carlos turned to face him.

"We're here," he said, gesturing out the window.

Carlos looked to his right and watched as they passed through a slowly opening gate and up a long driveway.

"*Bienvenidos a Hacienda del Mar!*" said Ramirez, preceding Alice and Carlos from the car once Pedro had opened the door.

"I know he's a jerk, but be nice," hissed Alice as she scooted by Carlos.

He sighed, following her through the door and into the hot evening. Getting his bearings for a moment, he realized that they were at the top of a steep hill. An enormous rambling mansion was to his left, and before him were the twinkling lights of Ponce and the Caribbean beyond. He had to admit, it was breathtaking.

"Mr. Ramirez!" exclaimed Alice. "What a striking view!"

"Only enhanced by your beauty now that you're here," he said, putting his arm around her shoulders again. "And it's Eduardo, please. Certainly we're close enough friends for first names, *querida?*"

His tone was suggestive to an extreme and made Carlos narrow his eyes protectively, even as his brain hinted that something was off.

Close friends? After one business meeting?

While he'd been telling the truth about Latinos being touchy-feely two nights ago when Alice had been jealous of Ana María, something about Ramirez's attentions just didn't feel right. It was almost as though he had an *expectation* of more-than-business from Alice. Why?

"Shall we change for dinner?" suggested Ramirez, turning to Pedro and telling him in Spanish to bring in the luggage, after which he could *return* the car and go home. "And then I would love to take you on a *private* tour of the grounds, Alice."

Alice demurred, saying something about freshening up being a good idea as she and Carlos followed a maid, dressed in a traditional black-and-white uniform, up a flight of stairs. She showed Alice to her room first, then asked Carlos to follow her to the end of the hallway, where she opened another door and told him she hoped he'd be comfortable.

Carlos considered walking back down the hall to Alice's room, but instead he opened his suitcase and unpacked a dress shirt and some crisp khaki pants, changing quickly. Nothing felt quite right since they'd arrived: Ramirez's manner was too familiar, too entitled, and Carlos didn't like it, but where had it come from? Also, he didn't understand why Ramirez had hired a driver and rented a car for a ten-minute ride from the airport to his home. Was that maid who'd showed him to his room an employee of Ramirez's? Or just another local hired to make a certain impression?

As he buttoned his shirt, his phone dinged, and he grabbed it from the bed.

LETICIA: Where are we going on Friday? I want to figure out what to wear.

Carlos' eyes widened as he stared at the text.

Fuck. Fuck, fuck, fuck.

Lena was going to kill him, but there was no way he was going out with another girl.

CARLOS: Sorry. I'm not going to be able to make it on Friday.

LETICIA: Still away on business? Saturday works for me.

He flinched. How honest should he be?

Honest enough that if Alice ever saw his phone, she'd feel satisfied with his answer. He loved Lena. He loved all of his family. But Carlos was with Alice now, and nothing—not even his family—could change that.

CARLOS: I'm really sorry, but I'm not going to be able to take you out. I'm with someone else now.

LETICIA: …

LETICIA: …

LETICIA: YOU ARE A FUCKING ASSHOLE.

LETICIA: DON'T EVER CONTACT ME AGAIN, HIJO DE PUTA!

A barrage of messages joined that one, and Carlos had no other option but to block Leticia's number. *Mierda*, Lena was going to let him have it when he got home. Oh, well, he hoped that she'd understand once he explained everything. There was no going back from what he had with Alice. He loved her. That's all there was to it.

Which meant that he needed to figure out a way for them to be together. He knew that Alice would offer to remove herself from SST if that's what it took for them to stay together. But he couldn't let her do that. Part of the reason that he hadn't wanted to leave his present position at SST was because it was the only way for him to see Alice every day and take care of her. But if they were a couple? He could see and take care of her out of the office. Which meant that he would be free to pursue a different dream that he'd been on the fence about for quite some time: applying to Wharton. The benefit of this plan, of course, was that when he graduated with an MBA, he could work *with* Alice instead of *for* her.

Heading downstairs, he paused at Alice's door for a moment but decided against knocking. If he was alone with her, even if it was to share his decision to apply to grad school, he'd be distracted the second he laid eyes on her. He'd reach for her. He wouldn't be able to stop himself; he'd be cock-deep inside of her three minutes later. The best he could hope for was that tonight, once their host had gone to bed, he could sneak into her room and spend the rest of the night with his hand over her mouth making her come.

As he came to the bottom of the stairs, the same maid who showed them to their room passed him, and he asked her in Spanish where he could find Ramirez. She shrugged and kept walking.

Carlos turned one way, only to find himself in a large, empty room that looked like some sort of secondary living room. It was dark and had only a lonely sofa against the wall. He turned and went the other direction, finding Ramirez in a den-like room with leather chairs and an enormous flat-screen TV.

"*Hola*," he said. Then remembering Alice's admonition, he added, "Your house is very beautiful."

Ramirez reached for the remote and turned off the TV, then stood and faced Carlos. "All settled in?"

"*Sí. Gracías.*"

"Drink?"

"Thanks," he said, stepping farther into the room.

"You're, uh, very clever," said Ramirez in English, pouring some amber-colored liquor into two glasses. "My assistant doesn't make mistakes. You *chose* not to make a hotel reservation."

Carlos didn't answer, just eyed Ramirez as he offered Carlos the glass.

"It's rum."

"Thank you," said Carlos, taking a sip.

"So," said Ramirez, perching on the arm of the couch, "things have certainly changed between you and your boss since we met in Philly last week, eh?"

"How do you mean?"

"Last week, you *wanted* to fuck her. This week, you *have*."

Carlos flinched, lowering his glass. His voice was a flinty growl. "Insult her again, and I will flatten you, Ramirez. I don't care whether or not this is your home. I won't let you talk about her like that."

"I really don't mean any disrespect," he said, taking another sip of his drink. "Though I do wonder…"

"What do you wonder?"

"Which one of us she's playing."

"Playing?" he asked, feeling warm. No, feeling murderous.

"Does it bother you that your woman was coming on to another man?"

He stared at Ramirez, wanting to punch him in the face, but something about what he was saying didn't feel entirely wrong or untrue, and it just about made Carlos want to be sick.

"What the fuck are you talking about?"

"Oh, ho ho ho," chuckled Ramirez. "*Probrecito. No lo sabes, eh?*" Poor thing. You don't know, huh?

"*Sabes…que?*" Know what?

Ramirez placed his glass on an end table, plucked his

phone from his back pocket, and read his texts: "'*Eduardo, I do hope we will become far better acquainted during my time in Puerto Rico...and not just as business associates.*'" He looked up quizzically. "Or this one...'*I could do far worse for myself than a handsome Puerto Rican.*'" He chuckled again. "Except she wrote that to me, not you." He scrolled through his messages, then stopped at another. "'*Oh, you are naughty, Eduardo, but naughty is a lot more fun...after dark.*'" He turned the phone around, holding it up for Carlos' inspection. "Want to take a look? There are a bunch more."

"No," hissed Carlos, throwing back the entire contents of his glass.

"Gentlemen."

Carlos jerked his head around to find Alice standing in the doorway of the den, looking so crazy beautiful, it made his heart clutch.

There were two things he needed to know:

One, when had she exchanged those fucking texts with Ramirez? And two, why?

***

"*Querida,*" said Ramirez, "you are a vision in blue this evening. Why, I could almost—" His phone rang, cutting off his speech. He looked down at it and frowned. "I need to take this. You'll excuse me? Your helper can get you a drink."

Walking from the room, Alice lifted her gaze to Carlos, who looked...

Furious.

"Carlos?" she said, walking over to him and placing her hand on his bare arm.

When she'd dressed tonight, she'd only thought of him—of how she longed to find herself back in his arms, of how long it had been since he'd told her he loved her, of how hard she would work to find a solution for the problem of them working together. She knew that it had bothered him to see Ramirez acting so familiarly, but the first chance she got, she'd planned to tell Ramirez that the texts were a mistake and that she was no longer available.

The look on his face made her wonder if she was too late.

"On Thursday morning, on the way to the airport, you were texting him, weren't you?"

"Shiiit," she murmured.

The last thing—*the very last thing* she'd ever want to do was hurt him.

"Wow," he said, shaking his head, his face taken aback and hurt. "Okay. So it's true."

"I was trying to convince myself he was a better match."

"Than me."

"No! Well…yes," she admitted, feeling miserable. "But we weren't together yet. I was just scared—"

"He's a pompous, entitled, smarmy little shit with three ex-wives. Is that what you want? To be number four?"

"Please, Carlos…that was before—"

"You need to figure out what you want, Alice."

"I *know* what I want, and I want—"

"Hi."

They whipped their heads to the side to find a little boy standing in the doorway, holding a soccer ball.

"H-Hi," said Alice. "Ah-hem. You are…?"

"Ricardo Ramirez," he said, holding out his hand to her. "*Mucho gusto.*"

Frustrated that she couldn't continue her conversation with Carlos, she had no choice but to take the little boy's hand. She mustered a smile for him. "It's nice to meet you.

I'm Miss Story."

"*Sí*, I know. My *papá* told me to be on my best behavior and maybe I would have a new step*mamá* soon."

Alice blinked at the child, her shock making speech impossible.

Carlos cleared his throat meaningfully, raising an eyebrow at Alice.

"I think—I think your father has oversold the situation," she said, lifting her chin. "I am not in the market to be someone's stepmother." Reviewing her words, she hurried to reassure him that her feelings weren't personal. "I mean—if I was, you seem like a terrific…well, you're a very polite child. Ummm…" She turned to Carlos. "Help?"

He rolled his eyes at her before turning to Ricardo.

"*Hey, muchacho, quieres jugar un poco antes de cenar?*"

"*Sí! Mi papa nunca tiene tiempo para jugar!*"

"*No me sorpresa,*" said Carlos dryly, opening his hands for the ball, which Ricardo threw to him with a gap-toothed grin. The child ran outside, and Carlos started to follow, then turned around and grabbed Alice around the waist with one strong arm. He hauled her against his chest and kissed her hard, like he was branding her or punishing her a little. "*Don't* play with me."

She wilted against him, wanting to cry with regret and relief. "I'm not. I swear."

"We'll see."

He released her with a cross look, then followed the child out a set of open French doors that led to a bright-green lawn adjacent to an aqua swimming pool.

She looked around the den, her sights falling to the recessed bar beside the massive TV, and she approached it to fix herself a drink. Opening the cupboard, she found it bare, but on the counter was a bottle of very good rum, so she poured herself a glass and then turned toward the patio by the grassy lawn where Carlos and Ricardo were playing a pickup game of soccer.

He was good with the boy, she realized, squatting down to give him tips and encouraging him when they started playing again. At one point Ricardo scored a goal on Carlos, and he hoisted the little boy on his shoulders and ran a victory lap around the lawn.

"I see the children have found each other."

Alice turned to see Eduardo approaching.

"Carlos isn't a child," she said.

Eduardo smiled at her indulgently. "But he is *much* younger than us."

Her cheeks flushed, and she took another sip of her rum, watching Carlos and Ricardo.

"Now you and I? That's what I call a perfect match," he said, running a finger slowly down her bare arm.

Alice stepped away from him, giving him a haughty look as his finger froze in midair. "I'm sorry if I misled you."

"Misled me? Not at all. You were *very clear* that you were open to more than a business relationship with me."

Carlos, who was within earshot, threw the ball to Ricardo, then turned to look at Alice, his dark eyes searching her face, waiting to hear her answer. Her heart flooded with love for him, stronger and more certain than any feeling she'd ever known, and she turned to Eduardo, lifting her chin and narrowing her eyes.

"Circumstances have changed. I'm no longer interested."

"*Amorcito*," he said, "it's fine with me if you want to go slumming for a little while. I don't mind waiting."

Carlos stopped the ball that Ricardo kicked his way but then straightened up and advanced on Eduardo. Alice stepped quickly in front of him, her back flush against his chest.

"I'm with Carlos now, señor."

"Ah," he said, his smile humorless as he stared at them. "But for how long?"

"For as long as he'll have me," she said softly.

Carlos' arms encircled her waist from behind, resting, one over the other, on her stomach. The gesture was possessive, and she welcomed it, leaning back into him, feeling his forgiveness wash over her like a soothing breeze on a scorching day.

Eduardo nodded. "I see."

"That said," Alice continued, "we are here to discuss business. And I dearly hope our conversations will be fruitful. I am no less interested in your vineyard proposition."

"Dinner is served, señor," announced the maid, standing between the open French doors and ringing a small brass bell.

"*Bueno*," said Eduardo, his face unaccountably stony, given her remaining enthusiasm about their business venture. "We may as well eat."

***

Ramirez sat at the head of the table, sucking down rum like it was going out of style and jumping down his son's throat every time the boy asked a question, which was making Carlos' already hot temper fiery.

Several times, Alice tried to engage him in conversation about the vineyards in *Bahía de Plata* or about the possible joint venture in Ponce, but Ramirez was an asshole, responding with one-word answers as he gestured for the maid to keep filling his glass.

They had started with *salmorejo*, a cold crab and tomato

soup, and the maid had just served a salad of octopus with a citrus vinaigrette and tropical fruit when Carlos' phone rang. He ignored it until it started ringing again. Pulling it from his pocket, he saw that it wasn't Lena or Leticia calling as he'd assumed, but Shane.

"Will you excuse me?" he asked his surly host, who gestured for him to go as he threw back yet another glass of rum.

Carlos gave Alice a grim smile before leaving the dining room and returning to the patch of lawn where he and Ricardo had been playing.

"Shane?"

"Carlos! Thank goodness! I tried Alice four or five times, but I don't think she has her phone with her."

"Is everything okay?" he asked.

"Here, yes. There? No."

"What do you mean?"

"I played eighteen holes with my friend Skip Jones and his father, William, over at Bryn Mawr Country Club today. When I mentioned our possible vineyard venture in Ponce, William answered that he'd gone to Wharton with a fellow from Puerto Rico whom, he'd learned, had fallen on hard times. I asked for the name of his friend, and you can imagine my shock when he said Eduardo Ramirez."

Carlos flinched, looking over his shoulder before asking. "What else?"

"Well, it seems that our Mr. Ramirez is not a winning bet and hasn't been in quite some time, though he's still managing the appearance of success. William said that he'd almost been 'taken for a ride' by Ramirez but backed out of a deal at the last minute. Some of his friends weren't so lucky."

"What kind of deal?"

"It seemed he was trying to start a rum business."

Carlos nodded, his fury mounting. "What does he want with Alice?"

"What do you think?" asked Shane. "No doubt her fortune."

"Asshole!"

"Yeah. I looked into him further, Carlos. Yes, he purchased some land in Ponce a few months ago, but it's already been repossessed by the bank. Though there may have been a plan to start a vineyard at one time, Ramirez is broke. I mean, way overextended. He's going to declare bankruptcy any day now."

Carlos thought about the driver and rented limo, the living room with a lonely sofa, the maid who didn't appear to know the layout of his house. This visit was a sham, just a big play to try to impress Alice and get into her pants—or her bank account.

"Priscilla's beside herself," said Shane. "I guess she and Margaret were really pressuring Alice to go for him."

"Don't worry."

"Are you sure? Pris said something about her e-mailing him or—"

"I'm sure, Shane. I'll take care of it."

There was a short pause before Shane said, "Of her."

"Always."

"I knew it!" exclaimed Shane. "You two are—"

"Figuring things out," he said quickly. "Not a word to Priscilla, huh?"

Shane chuckled good-naturedly. "Don't worry."

"You knew?"

"Suspected." Shane paused. "The way you say her name…it feels different. The way a man calls to the woman he loves…like how I call Priscilla 'P. But Pris told me I was wrong."

"You weren't."

"You'll protect her?"

"With my life."

Carlos could feel Shane's smile when he responded. "I know she's in good hands."

"I should go back to dinner. Alice's all alone in there," said Carlos, but then he remembered something: the solution to the problem of him and Alice working together. "Shane, can you do me a favor?"

"Of course. Name it."

"In my desk. Bottom drawer. In the back…"

"Yeah…"

"There's a large envelope, stamped and addressed. It's my admission packet for Wharton. Can you send it in for me?"

"So you decided to go for it, huh? Damn, that's good news!"

"Don't get too excited. I'm a long shot. I'll be competing against guys from Yale and Harvard."

"Yeah, well, none of them have a recommendation from me!"

Carlos chuckled. "True enough."

"You started SST with Alice from scratch. They'll be panting for you. No worries. I'll send it first thing tomorrow."

"Thanks, Shane. For that…and for calling me."

"Take care of her, okay?"

"You know it," he said. "Bye."

Pressing the end button his phone, he stood on the grass under the stars for two minutes, breathing in the air of his home country as he tried to figure out the best course of action. God damn it, this guy had been nothing but trouble from the start.

Carlos entered the dining room and took his seat, turning to Alice. "What did I miss?"

"We were just talking about the vineyards. The land isn't far from here," she said. "Eduardo said he could take us to see it in the morning, and we can talk about our investment."

Carlos sat back in his chair, eyeing Ramirez, the dirty, cheating snake.

"You know?" said Carlos. "I'd like to see a survey of the land after dinner. Certainly you have one?"

Ramirez sneered. "It's at my lawyer's office. Safer there."

"Hmm," hummed Carlos, taking a sip of rum, no doubt the result of Ramirez's last failed venture. "Then let's stop at your lawyer's office first thing? Before we visit the actual plot of land? We can look at the survey then."

"I don't even know if—well, I mean, my lawyer could be out of town."

"Surely he has an assistant who could accommodate your request? You have investors in town who want to see a survey. I'm sure they'd be only happy to—"

"You're very presumptuous," said Ramirez, turning back to Alice. "My business is with Miss Story, not you."

"Actually," said Carlos, "your business isn't with anyone, is it? I mean, no one reputable, anyway. There is no land, is there?"

Alice jerked her head to look at him, her brows furrowed. "Carlos! What are you—?"

"*Quien eres tú? Un puto campesino!* You have no right to grill me with questi—"

"You are a cheat and a liar! I should *beat* you!"

The maid tapped Ricardo on the shoulder, taking his hand and leading him into the kitchen.

"For what? For not wanting to share my holdings with Miss Story's coffee boy? You're out of your league, *muchacho! Callaté tu boca* and let the grown-ups talk!"

"What in the world is going on here?" demanded Alice, staring back and forth between the two men in shock.

Carlos turned to Alice. "That was Shane on the phone with a warning." He shot a disgusted glance at Ramirez, gesturing to him with a flick of his chin. "He's in debt up to his ears. There's no land. No vineyard. Only a desperate man hoping to land a rich girl."

Alice turned to look at Ramirez, her mouth opened in dismay. "Is this true?"

"Miss Story. Alice. We are cut from the same cloth, you and me. Ivy League schools. The best of everything. If anyone's a fortune hunter here, it's this *pendejo* who follows you around like a fucking puppy."

Alice flattened her hands and banged them on the table, standing slowly and staring down Ramirez with eyes like daggers.

"How *dare* you?" she spat. "A fortune hunter? Ha! He trusted me when I had *nothing* to offer. This man," she said, laying her hand on Carlos' shoulder, "this beautiful, smart, talented man is the very last person in the world you could accuse of being a fortune hunter! Furthermore, if I'm cut from *any* cloth on earth, *please, God*, let it be from his, because he is loyal and honest and true. If he says you're a schemer, you're a schemer. If he says you're garbage…you're garbage." She squeezed Carlos' shoulder, and he stood up beside her, looking down at his fierce, righteous, brilliant woman and thanking every star in the sky that he'd gambled everything on her once upon a time. "Carlos, my love…is Mr. Ramirez garbage?"

"*Sí, mi amor*," he said. "Total and complete *basura*."

"Good enough for me," said Alice, pushing her chair away from the table and stepping around it. She offered Carlos her hand, and he took it, raising it to his lips and pressing a kiss to it.

"Let's get packed and get out of here," he suggested.

"Sounds like a plan." She nodded, letting him lead her from the room.

"You deserve each other!" yelled Ramirez, throwing his half-drunk glass of rum in their direction, the tumbler nailing Alice in the ass and the contents spilling down the back of her blue dress. She gasped in shock, trying to look over her shoulder at the mess.

Carlos dropped her hand, pivoted, and advanced on Ramirez with unrestrained fury. "I told you I'd deck you if you ever disrespected Miss Story in front of me again."

He grabbed Ramirez by the collar of his white polo shirt, drew back his fist, slammed it into Ramirez's face, and then dropped him back onto his chair with a split lip.

"And treat your kid with a little more fucking kindness, *pendejo puto.*"

Finished taking out the trash, he strode toward Alice, took her outstretched hand, and escorted her from the room.

Chapter 12

Alice's alarm went off at five o'clock the next morning as usual, but she reached for it and silenced it, placing it gently back on the hotel nightstand.

Rolling onto her side, she sighed, her lips tilting up into a smile as she gazed at Carlos, naked on his back, a white sheet pulled up to his hips, his beautiful chest bare.

For a moment, just a moment, her breath caught in amazement.

Last night, for a few terrifying seconds, she'd had a glimpse of her life without him in it when he'd warned her to "figure out" what she wanted. It had been crystal clear to her then: he was all that she wanted. Him. Carlos Vega. She loved him...more.

More than her family.

More than her company.

More than her ambition.

More than anything.

After knowing what it was to love and be loved by him, life would be meaningless without him.

"I feel you lookin' at me, baby." Caught, she gasped, her smile widening as he cracked open one eye to look at her. He grinned at her, his other eye opening. "Good morning, Miss Story."

"Good morning, Mr. Vega," she said, leaning forward to rest her breasts against his chest and press her lips to his for a gentle kiss.

He reached up, cupping her cheeks. "You want to go for a run?"

She shook her head. "No. Not yet. I'm too comfortable."

"Is there anything I can do to make you *more* comfortable, *mi amor*?" he asked, his voice a low purr.

"I can think of a few things," she said, her clit throbbing for the touch of his tongue, "but first, I'm going to take care of you."

She leaned down, pressing her lips to his chest, trailing them lower, over the ridges of muscle to his stomach. Wedging her knee between his legs, she repositioned herself, straddling his thigh with her exposed sex and leaning down to lick his cock from base to tip.

"Put it in your mouth," he told her, his voice gritty with need as he flexed the muscles in his thigh to massage her clit.

Alice wound her tongue around the head of his erection, licking the salty precum from the tip.

"All the way," he demanded, reaching for her head and gathering her hair in his hands.

She clutched the base of his cock in her hand and lowered her mouth over the hard shaft until he hit the back of her throat. His hands guided her movements tightly, urging her to slide her lips back up the rigid column and then pushing her head back down, and she found that submitting to his will gave her a certain freedom she wouldn't have expected. With other lovers, she'd overthought everything she was doing, which had made her uptight, living in her own head instead of being *in* the moment.

With Carlos, because of their established trust and the way he took control, she was able to escape her head, her worries, her expectations...he was giving her the gift of immediacy, and she reveled in the brazenness of it. She could abandon herself to his will, to the sound of his voice, to sensation and feeling. For the first time in her life, she could be uncontrolled and unrestrained. Here, in this sacred place where he loved her and she loved him, pleasuring each other was a bold act of faith without second-guesses, without fear, and without reservation.

"You're going to swallow what I give you, *mi amor*," he said, his grip tightening on her hair. "Understand?"

"Mm-hm," she murmured, swirling her tongue around his twitching, pulsing cock before deep throating him again, chills sliding down her back from the sound of his deep, satisfied groan.

Remembering the way his teeth on her clit had made her explode yesterday, she looked up at him, at the way his face had started to contort in earnest, his eyes clenched shut. He was holding her hair so tightly it hurt, but in a good way, an intense way. Sliding his cock all the way out of her mouth, she placed her teeth tentatively on the base of his shaft and dragged them up his length, chasing the sharpness with her tongue.

"Fuck, Allie!" he cried as his hips bucked off the bed.

She clamped her lips over the tip of his erection and slid them back down just as he burst, streams of his seed sliding down the back of her throat in hot pulses.

"God," he hissed, his hand loosening in her hair. "Fuck, that was...intense. Fuck, baby."

Releasing him inch by inch, she pressed her lips to the tip of his cock in a sweet kiss and then rolled to her side, pressing up against him in bed.

His arm landed loosely on her hip as he slowly opened his eyes and turned his head to the side. "You're a goddess."

She chuckled. "I'm good at following directions."

"Yes, you are, baby," he said, bending his neck to kiss her. "That was...crazy hot."

Alice grinned, making lazy circles in his chest as her own body, wet and primed, waited for him to tell her he was ready for more.

"Allie?"

"Hmm?"

"You know what I want to do today?" he asked, running his fingers up and down her back.

"What?"

"I want to..." He sighed, knowing that a case could be made for them moving too fast. But it felt right. *So* right. He started again. "I want to introduce you to my mom and dad."

She snapped her head up, bracing on her elbow. "You want me to meet your family?"

He blinked at her, his eyes wide. "Yeah. Is that a problem?"

"We've only been together for two days!"

"So what?" he said, pushing her hair from her face as he gazed at her. "I love you. I love them. I want you to know each other." He guided her lips to his and kissed her tenderly. "And, baby, we've been together a *lot* longer than two days. We've just gotten around to the good stuff in the last two days, but *this*—everything between us? It's been growing for years."

"Yes, but—"

"Allie," he said, leaning up on his elbow to mirror her, "be straight with me. When we get home, do you want to be together?"

"Yes! But I don't—"

"You don't quite know how it's going to work yet?"

"Exactly."

"Do you trust me?"

She nodded. "With everything I am."

"Can you trust me that this is day two of forever?"

Her eyes filled with tears, and she nodded, unable to speak over the lump in her throat.

"Can you trust me that we'll figure out everything?"

She nodded again, leaning forward to rest her forehead on his.

"Can you come and meet my parents today?"

"Of course," she whispered. "Thank you."

"For what?"

"For showing me how to do this."

"This?"

"Love someone. Be loved. Let it happen."

"I told you the first night, baby," he said, pressing his lips to hers, "once we were together, I was never walking away, and I would never let you go."

She sniffled softly. "I know. I just—"

He rolled onto his back, reaching for her waist and pulling her onto his chest. "Have I ever said something to you that wasn't true?"

Alice straddled his chest with her knees and leaned back a little, feeling his erection, stiff and waiting, press against her. "Never."

"Trust me, Allie," he said. "Yeah?"

"Yeah," she murmured, lifting a little to position herself over him.

"Good. Now ride me."

He reached down and gripped his cock, holding it steady so she could slide down onto it, inch by hot, swollen inch.

He fills me. Dear God, how he fills me.

And not just her body, which sucked him forward, fitting around his thickness like a custom-made glove, but her heart too, which sang with pleasure, knowing real and true love for the first time in her lonely life.

He held her hips as she surged forward, then back. Forward, then back, riding him like he'd asked her too, his gray eyes looking so deeply into hers, she felt her body flush at the same time she felt the tightening of her muscles. And in the end, when they found their sweet release, they found it together, intimately joined by their bodies.

Their eyes.

And their hearts.

***

Carlos had made the drive from Ponce to San Juan many times, as Ponce was the site of the annual *Liga Atlética Interuniversitaria de Puerto Rico*—essentially a week of sporting events between island universities, and he had played soccer for his own college up near San Juan. And frankly, even if a college student wasn't on a sports team, most of them still went down to Ponce to cheer on their alma mater and party every night. So most of the drives he'd made from Ponce north found him hung over and exhausted after a week of hard playing and hard partying. But not today. Today was different. Today he was taking the love of his life home to meet his parents.

As they cruised along the roads that snaked through the interior of his island, he glanced over at her. Because she'd only packed business and workout clothes, they'd visited the lobby boutique in their hotel, and Alice had chosen a peach-colored sundress, decorated with white palm fronds, and simple white sandals. She put her hair in a ponytail, and her sunburn from two days ago had turned into a deep tan. Carlos had never seen her so beautiful, though he liked to think that his love for her, and the manifestation of that love in a two-day fuckfest, had something to do with the way she was suddenly blooming.

"What?" she asked.

"Nothin'," he said, turning back to the road.

"Tell me!"

He grinned at her, glancing over once more. "You just look really...beautiful."

Over the last few days, he'd gotten more accustomed to her easy smiles, but this one held so much happiness, so much promise, that it was lucky they were on a deserted road because he swerved a little, drinking it in.

"Careful!" she cautioned him.

"Then quit smilin' like that."

"I can't," she said with a happy sigh. "I can't help it."

She reached over and put her hand on his thigh. "Why do you think it took us so long to admit our feelings for each other?"

He took one hand off the steering wheel, took her hand, and raised it to his lips for a quick kiss. "I think it took as long as it needed to. We had to be ready. Things can happen very fast when two people are ready."

"You're telling me!" she joked, letting go of his hand to grab her bottle of water from the console between them. She uncapped it and took a long sip before replacing it. "I've never been with anyone like you."

"Tall, dark, and Latino?" he asked. "Once you go Boricua, you'll never go back, *mi amor*."

She giggled. "No worries there. I'm not going anywhere."

"You've had boyfriends, Alice," he said thoughtfully.

"Yes, but I never trusted any of them." She paused. "I never loved any of them."

He glanced over at her slipping smile. "Who *do* you love?"

He heard her take a deep breath and hold it, like maybe the question hurt a little.

"I'll say names," he suggested, "and you can nod if the answer's yes."

"Okay."

"Margaret."

She nodded quickly.

"Elizabeth."

She pursed her lips but nodded again.

"Priscilla."

Another nod.

"Jane."

"Jane," she said softly. "Everyone loves Jane. Wait 'til you get to know her. She's a saint, Carlos."

"*Santa Juana*," he said.

"She finished med school in June. She's…I mean, she's a pediatrician. She saves kids. For a living. How amazing do you have to be to choose that for your life's work?"

"Very," he said, loving the warmth in her voice as she spoke of her little sister.

"What about Elizabeth? What's going on with her?"

"She's up my father's ass like a colon polyp."

"Nice," he said, nodding in appreciation of Alice's saltier side.

"It's true. She's…insufferable lately. When we were girls, she was the rebel, you know? Smoking with boys, stealing liquor from my parent's cabinet. She was fun! Chunky and irreverent and real…and such a good time. Somewhere along the way, she changed. And now she's this plastic Barbie doll who follows my father around like a servant."

"But he promoted her," Carlos observed carefully.

"Yes," said Alice bitterly.

"After passing you and Margaret over."

"Yes," she said more softly.

"That must be difficult."

She nodded. "It doesn't feel great."

He pulled the car to the side of the road, put it in park, turned to her, and said, "Your father."

Her jaw tightened, and she sucked in a small breath, staring at her folded hands on her lap. Finally, she shrugged. "I don't know. He's my father. I *should* love him. But…"

"Fuck all the 'shoulds,' Alice. You let them rule your life." He paused, softening his voice. "I know you don't hate him, but do you love him?"

"I wish I could answer you," she said. "But I honestly don't know."

Carlos winced. "He betrayed you."

"By not promoting me?"

"By making you feel unloved," said Carlos, reaching out to cup her cheek as her eyes filled with tears. "His first and most important job was to love his children. If he fails at that, he fails at everything."

She sniffled, and he used his thumb to wipe away a lone tear.

"Are you saying…it's him, not me?" she asked, trying for a little levity and missing the mark.

"I'm saying…you're so easy to love, Allie. I'm sorry that he's missing his chance."

A shudder tore through her, and she turned her head, pressing her lips into his palm as he asked, "Carlos?"

She looked up at him, nailing him with her eyes, and

nodded.

"Yes," she said, her face brightening, her smile like watching the sun break through the clouds on a rainy day. "I love him."

"He loves you too."

She pulled his hand from her cheeks and braided her hands through him, settling both in her lap as he switched gears and stepped on the gas.

***

"Ready to meet my family?" Carlos asked, turning into a parking space in a lot beside *Casa Vega*, his family's restaurant.

"Run through the names with me again?" asked Alice, eyeing the colorful restaurant nervously. She wanted them to like her, but she couldn't remember the last time she'd been taken home to meet someone's family. And certainly no time before had ever counted as much as this one.

"You're just stalling now."

"Please," she said. "One more time."

He nodded. "My parents are Pablo and Elena."

"And they speak English?"

"It's not their first language, but yes." He smiled at her. "My younger brother, Francisco, will be there working, and his wife, Luisa, sometimes comes in for a few hours with their son, Carlitos."

"Named after you."

"Sí," he said, grinning at her. "My youngest brother, Pablo, named after my father, is called Paco. It's a nickname. He's not engaged or married, so no one else to remember with him."

"And your sister is Carmela."

"*Exactamente.* And she's engaged to…?"

"Umm…" hummed Alice, tapping her chin. "Mike."

"Sí, Mike. From Miami."

"Why isn't Mike called Miguel?"

Carlos shrugged. "'Cause he's not *Puertorriqueño, querida.* He's a *gringo*, like you."

"Gringo?"

"Not *Latino*. He's Irish, I think. Freckles and red hair," said Carlos. "You'll know him when you see him."

"Anyone else I should know about?"

"Baby, I got about a hundred cousins, aunts, and uncles...my *abuelos*—that's grandparents—won't be there because they live in San Juan...but I think knowing my immediate family is enough, huh?"

Alice gulped nervously, but she nodded, offering him a small smile.

"I'll be right next to you the whole time, *mi amor.* Trust me?"

He leaned over the bolster of the rental car, cupped her cheek, and kissed her soundly, only stopping at the sharp knock on the window.

"Hey, Carlos! *Eres tú? Quien es ella?*" *Hey, Carlos! Is that you? Who's she?*

Carlos laughed softly against Alice's lips, looking up at her. "Paco." Then he turned and opened his door, stepping out of the car only to be enveloped in a bear hug by a young man almost twice his size.

Smiling at their exuberance, Alice opened her own door and rounded the car to stand to the side.

When the brothers leaned away from each other, Carlos grabbed Alice's hand.

"Alice, this is my *little* brother, Paco. Paco, meet Alice."

"Ha! Little? I was taller than you two years ago!"

Carlos turned to Alice. "He's the forward of his high school basketball team."

Alice held out her hand. "It's so nice to meet you."

"You too," said Paco. "What are you doing with this *pendejo*? You're too pretty for him!"

"I know," she said, "but he looked so lonely, I took pity on him."

Paco laughed, nodding with appreciation. "Oh, shoot! I like her! She's got some spirit, yeah?"

Carlos chuckled. "She's gonna be around for a while, so I'm glad you approve. Is *Mami* here?"

"Come on, *Carlitos Uno*," he said, throwing a bag of garbage in a dumpster before herding them into the back door of the restaurant. "Where else would she be?"

Three hours later, Alice had been offered more food than she'd ever seen in her entire life, drunk her weight in cold beer, and been thoroughly embraced by the entire Vega clan, right down to *Carlitos Dos*, Carlos' two-year-old namesake, who was, at present, taking a nap in Carlos' lap. Pablo and Elena were back in the kitchen prepping for dinner, Francisco and Carmela were waiting tables, and Paco was bussing. Luisa, who'd run across the street to the CVS to grab something for her son, would be back any minute.

"He's beautiful," said Alice, staring at his lips, slack with sleep.

"Sí," agreed Carlos, running a gentle hand through his nephew's down-like hair. "And he's a good baby too."

"I…" Alice bit her bottom lip. "I don't suppose you're anywhere near ready to—"

"To have my own? Are you kidding, *querida*? I can't wait!"

"But you're so young," she said. "It'll be years before you're ready."

"Francisco is my *younger* brother!" exclaimed Carlos. "I always wanted to be a young dad, and my brother's already got one! No, Allie. I have no interest in waiting. I'm ready whenever you are, *mami*."

"Are you serious?"

Luisa walked over to their table. "I'm gonna take him home now, Carlos. Thanks for keeping an eye on him."

Carlos lifted the sleeping child gently, transferring him to his mother's arms. "It was good to see you, Luisa."

"You too, *hermano*," she said, leaning down to kiss his cheek. "And it was good to meet you, Allie. Keep an eye on this one for me, huh?"

Alice nodded. "Won't let him out of my sight. I promise."

Luisa winked at them, then hurried over to say good-bye to her husband.

Turning back to Alice, Carlos took her hand across the table. "Come with me."

He led her outside to a little garden adjacent to the restaurant that had hot-pink flowers and a small pond with koi fish.

"Yes, baby. I'm serious," he said, pulling her into his arms under the stars. "I know what I want. This isn't new, or hurried, or some *loco* idea that needs time to develop. I've lived and breathed with you for three years. I know you. And you know me. You are the love of my life, Alice Story. And whatever happens next, happens with you by my side, and me by yours."

"Forever?" she asked, the word slipping from her lips as she stared into his stunning gray eyes.

He nodded. "Forever, baby. I'll make it official as soon as we get home."

She stood on tiptoes, kissing him with abandon. She'd worried about their age differences, their background differences, and whether or not they both wanted children.

But he'd quelled all her fears, one by one, the only one remaining now, the biggest: how could they be together romantically if they worked together too?

"Um…" she hummed, drawing back to look up at him. "There's still the matter of—"

"Our working together."

"Yes," she said. "How do you do that? Finish my sentences?"

He kissed the tip of her nose and held her tightly against him.

"Remember those back-to-back desks?" he asked. "In our first office?"

"Of course."

"I figure we sat at those desks for ten hours a day, five days a week, for thirteen months before Priscilla's investment. You know how many hours that is?"

"How many?"

"Two thousand six hundred hours. That's how long we sat back to back. And, baby, I was fallin' in love with you every minute of every hour of every day."

"Carlos"—she said his name tenderly, reverently— "how does this work?"

"I resign," he said firmly.

"No! Absolutely not!" Everything inside of her rebelled against him giving up his job for her, especially when he'd done that once in his life already. "You *can't* quit. My company is yours too. It's *ours*. It always has been."

He nodded. "Fair enough. But if I want to be your partner, I need a better education."

"No! You're perfect. You don't need to change a thing—"

"Alice, *querida*," he said, cupping her cheeks and forcing her to look at him. "I applied to Wharton."

She heard the sound of screeching brakes in her head. "*What?*"

He nodded, a grin tipping up the corners of his mouth. "Shane wrote me a rec. I filled out the forms...and I—I applied to Wharton."

Her eyes were sparking with tears as she searched his face. "Are you serious?"

"My company offers tuition reimbursement," he said, shrugging nonchalantly, his grin growing wider.

"Are you serious?"

He nodded. "I am, baby. I'm gonna go back to school, and then you can hire me back...as your partner."

"Carlos! I'm so proud of you!" she cried, throwing her arms around his neck.

"Yeah?"

"Oh, my God, yes!"

"Think I'll get in?"

"If I have anything to say about it."

"No, baby. I do this on my own or not at all."

"*Sí*, Carlos," she said, smoothing his shirt like a dutiful fiancée but clearly with an agenda of her own.

"*Mujer*, you're going to be a load of trouble, aren't you?"

"Probably," she said. She cocked her head to the side. "Sure you want me?"

"I'm sure," he said, releasing her waist to cup her face, nuzzling her nose before kissing her. "*Corazon de mi corazon.* Heart of my heart. I want what I've wanted from the very beginning...*us.*"

Epilogue

Four months later

"*…brilla la estrella de pa-a-az. Brilla la estrella de paz,*" sang Carlos, finishing the second coat of white trim around the bedroom window as his iPod played his favorite Christmas carol, *Silent Night*, in Spanish.

Finished, he laid the brush in the paint tray and stood up, stretching one arm over his head and then the other.

"*Noche de paz, noche de amor…*"

Turning around slowly, he smiled at his work—crisp cream-colored walls and bright white trim. This was the last of four bedrooms in the old house that had needed to be repainted, and he'd gotten it finished just in time. With Christmas only nine days away and all of Alice's sisters coming on Christmas Eve to spend the holiday with them, he'd made it his personal mission to have all the rooms patched, freshly painted, and ready for company.

Besides, more guests were coming on her sisters' heels.

When he and Alice were married the second weekend of January, his parents, brothers, and sister would be coming up from *La Isla* to stay with them too.

He'd made his proposal official two weeks after they'd returned home from Puerto Rico with a small diamond ring resting on top of her morning latte, accompanied by the résumé from the young woman he'd hired to be his replacement.

Alice had tried to convince him to stay on and let her take a leave of absence instead, but he insisted he'd have his hands full. He'd spend a month training her replacement before announcing his resignation and their engagement, and then he'd concentrate on renovating their new house and taking care of any wedding-planning details that she couldn't see to. That was his number-one job and greatest pleasure, after all: taking care of Alice.

And taking care of her meant being together. The night they returned from Puerto Rico, they'd slept apart, in their own homes…and the next morning, they agreed that one night apart was more than enough for a lifetime and then locked her office door, pulled the blinds, and made up for lost time.

That weekend, Carlos broke his lease, and Alice put her downtown condo on the market so they could find a place of their own and move in together. A long day of house hunting had proved fruitful, and they'd found a reasonably priced, two-hundred-year-old farmhouse in Gladwyne, not far from Haverford…that required a lot of work. But Carlos was only too happy to roll up his sleeves and make it theirs, day by day, every day, patching plaster, painting walls, refinishing old wood floors, and replacing broken windows. It still needed work, but that was okay because he still had time.

In October, he heard from Wharton and was invited for an interview, which had raised his hopes considerably, and Alice had spent a good deal of time coaching him through the interview process. He was fairly certain that it had gone well, but he wouldn't know unless he received a letter. A letter that would have been posted two days ago on December 14.

"...*brilla sobre el Re-e-e-y. Brilla sobre el Rey.*"

Still humming, he folded up the paint drop cloth and gathered up the tape, paint, and brushes, taking everything down to the basement. He washed his hands in the ancient, stained basement sink, then threw on a barn jacket and walked in the dark down the snow-covered gravel driveway to the mailbox.

What if there was no letter there? Or what if there was a letter, but it expressed regret that there wasn't space for him in the upcoming class?

"Then you'll find a new job somewhere," he told himself, his stomach fluttering as he neared the mailbox. "And you can always reapply next year."

Opening the mailbox, he withdrew the small pile of Christmas cards and other envelopes, his heart stopping, then leaping when he found the envelope marked Wharton. He stared at it, wondering at its contents, knowing that his future—and Alice's—would be shaped by the letter inside and hoping against hope that it was a future they both wanted.

***

Alice's heart lifted, as it always did, when she got off the highway at Hollow Road.

Four minutes until I'm home.

They were the longest four minutes of her day, the drive from the highway to Carlos. But today they were longer than usual. Today there was wonderful news to be shared, and she couldn't wait to see his face when he found out what she already knew.

She pulled onto the driveway, parking her BMW in the gravel circle in front of the house. When they'd purchased it, the front stoop had required a good bit of masonry work. Luckily, one of Carlos' cousins in Philadelphia was a master mason and had spent several weekends out in Gladwyne helping his cousin fix and level the entry. More than once Carlos had taken off his shirt during long, hot afternoons of work, and she'd been certain to peek out the upstairs windows so she didn't miss his back muscles rippling in the sun.

She slipped her key in the lock and opened the front door, closing her eyes and inhaling the warm, wonderful smell of dinner, no doubt a recipe shared by Elena, with whom Alice had become very close over the last four months. They'd returned to Puerto Rico twice to visit with Carlos' family, and for the first time in Alice's life, she knew the gentle warmth of a mother figure. She couldn't wait to welcome Pablo and Elena to Pennsylvania in January.

"Carlos? Honey? I'm home!"

"In here, baby!" he called from the kitchen. "Just finishing up!"

She dropped her purse and laptop bag on the front table, took off her coat, and hung it in the front closet. Waiting for her were her favorite slippers, and she toed off her high heels and swapped them for homey comfort, then padded into the kitchen.

"It smells like heaven," she said, grinning at her fiancé.

"You *look* like heaven," said Carlos. "Come give me a kiss."

She crossed the kitchen to where he stood by the stove and stepped into his arms, opening her lips to his. He kissed her passionately, like they'd been gone for much longer than eight hours, making her weak in the knees, making her want to skip dinner and head straight to their waiting bed.

When he drew back, he grinned at her, then shook his head. "No, *mi amor*. Dinner first."

"Get out of my head!" she exclaimed, blinking at him in merriment.

"There's wine open on the table," he said, chuckling, "and this will be ready in two minutes."

Alice glanced at the table, and her eyes widened. In the center of the table, propped up, was an envelope from Wharton.

"It came!" she cried, snatching it up and holding it out to him. "Why haven't you opened it yet?"

"Because whatever it says, it affects both of us, Allie. I thought you should be here too." He turned off the stove, picked up the pot, and carried it to the table, placing it on a trivet.

"*Asopao?*" she asked, familiar with the Puerto Rican gumbo-style soup that Carlos made at least once a week for dinner.

"*Sí.* I was painting until four."

She sat down across from him and offered him the letter. "Time to open it."

He spooned some of the hearty soup into each of their bowls and looked up at her. "You do it."

"No," she said gently, still holding the letter out to him. "This is *your* news."

"*Bueno.*" He sighed, taking the letter from her and opening it while he held her eyes. "Whatever it says—"

"Whatever it says, we'll handle it together."

He nodded, removing the letter and unfolding it before dropping his eyes to read. Alice stared at him, trying to read his face, but it was frustratingly blank. "Well?"

Carlos looked up, a slow but steady smile blooming

across his face, his dimples denting his cheeks as he whispered, "I got in!"

She clapped her hands together and stood up, circling the small table and jumping into his lap. Wrapping her arms around his neck, she covered his face in kisses, both of them laughing with glee. The letter fluttered to the floor, and he held her tight, finding her lips with his, the kisses changing in an instant from celebratory to hot. He threaded his fingers into her hair as his tongue slid against hers, familiar and yet always new. How she loved him.

Finally, he drew away, still holding her cheeks with the palms of his hands. "So your husband's going to be a college student. You okay with that, *mami*?"

Alice gasped, searching his face, surprised by the endearment, which he used much less often than *mi amor* or *querida*.

His brow furrowed. "Alice? What is it?"

"About that…"

"Being a college student?"

She gulped, shaking her head slowly back and forth as her eyes filled with tears, because when all your dreams come true at once, it's hard to keep tears at bay.

"No. Um. I have some news to share too."

"Baby?" he asked, searching her eyes with worry, his smiling falling. "Are you all right?"

"Mm-hm." She felt her lips wobble into a smile as she bit her bottom lip.

"Then…?"

"It's going to be a busy year."

He nodded. "I don't start classes until September. We have plenty of time for fun before then."

"Mmm," she hummed, holding his eyes with hers, her smile blooming over her news just as his had blossomed over his. "If changing diapers is your idea of fun."

"Changing…" She watched his face transform as her news settled between them, his face changing from relaxed to disbelieving to joyful in the space of seconds. "Do you mean…?"

She nodded, giggling a little at his expression. "We're having a baby."

"Allie!" he cried, his hands slipping from her face to her flat belly. "You mean it?"

She grinned at him, wiping away the falling tears. "I'm due the last week in July."

"*Dios mio!*" he cried, pulling her close, resting his forehead on her shoulder as she rubbed his back and let the news settle in.

"You're going to be a dad, Carlos."

He leaned back, his eyes glistening with emotion as he reached up to cup her cheeks. "You're going to be the most beautiful mother, Allie. I love you. God, I love you so much!"

"I love you too," she whispered, leaning forward to nuzzle his nose with hers, to seal their future with a tender kiss. When she leaned away, her smile faded. "Except…"

"Here it comes," he said, shaking his head indulgently at her.

"A wedding. A new house. A baby. Grad school…" She bit her bottom lip. "How will we make it all work?"

"Ah-leese. Allie. *Querida. Mi amor. Mi cielo. Corazon de mi corazon.* How many times do I have to tell you? We're a team. There's *nothing* we can't figure out together."

She nodded, arching against him, needing him, their *asopao* forgotten as they kissed long and hard…and the learned lesson in Alice's joyful heart was this one:

The future isn't something perfect.

The future isn't something predictable.

The best thing you can do is find a partner who loves you and tackle it together.

THE END

Coming soon!

The Flirt and the Fox,
The Story Sisters #3
(Elizabeth Story and Merit Atwell's story)

The world of Blueberry Lane continues in 2017 with…

The Story Sisters

(Part IV of the Blueberry Lane Series)

The Bohemian and the Businessman

(Priscilla's story)

The Story Sisters #1

Available now!

The Director and Don Juan

(Alice's story)

The Story Sisters #2

Thank you for reading!

The Flirt and the Fox

(Elizabeth's story)

The Story Sisters #3

Coming in September 2017

Coming soon!

The Saint and the Scoundrel

(Jane's story)

The Story Sisters #4

Coming soon!

ALSO AVAILABLE
from Katy Regnery

a modern fairytale
(A collection)

THE BLUEBERRY LANE SERIES

THE ENGLISH BROTHERS
(Blueberry Lane Books #1–7)

THE WINSLOW BROTHERS
(Blueberry Lane Books #8–11)

Bidding on Brooks
Proposing to Preston
Crazy about Cameron
Campaigning for Christopher

THE ROUSSEAUS
(Blueberry Lane Books #12–14)

Jonquils for Jax
Marry Me Mad
J.C. and the Bijoux Jolis

THE STORY SISTERS
(Blueberry Lane Books #15–18)
Coming 2017

The Bohemian and the Businessman
The Director and Don Juan
The Flirt and the Fox
The Saint and the Scoundrel

THE AMBLERS
(Blueberry Lane Books #19–20)
Coming 2018

Belonging to Bree
Surrendering to Sloane

THE ATWELLS
(Blueberry Lane Books #21–24)
Coming 2019

Four books to be named

STAND-ALONE BOOKS:

After We Break

Frosted
(a romance novella for mature readers)

Four Weddings and a Fiasco: The Wedding Date
(a Kindle Worlds novella)

ABOUT THE AUTHOR

New York Times and USA Today bestselling author Katy Regnery started her writing career by enrolling in a short story class in January 2012. One year later, she signed her first contract, and Katy's first novel was published in September 2013.

Thirty books later, Katy claims authorship of the multititled *New York Times* and *USA Today* bestselling Blueberry Lane Series, which follows the English, Winslow, Rousseau, Story, and Ambler families of Philadelphia; the six-book, bestselling ~a modern fairytale~ series; and several other stand-alone novels and novellas.

Katy's first modern fairytale romance, *The Vixen and the Vet*, was nominated for a RITA® in 2015 and won the 2015 Kindle Book Award for romance. Katy's boxed set, *The English Brothers Boxed Set*, Books #1–4, hit the *USA Today* bestseller list in 2015, and her Christmas story, *Marrying Mr. English*, appeared on the list a week later. In May 2016, Katy's Blueberry Lane collection, *The Winslow Brothers Boxed Set*, Books #1–4, became a *New York Times* e-book bestseller.

In 2016, Katy signed a print-only agreement with Spencer Hill Press. As a result, her Blueberry Lane paperback books will now be distributed to brick-and-mortar bookstores all over the United States.

Katy lives in the relative wilds of northern Fairfield County, Connecticut, where her writing room looks out at the woods, and her husband, two young children, two dogs, and one Blue Tonkinese kitten create just enough cheerful chaos to remind her that the very best love stories begin at home.

Sign up for Katy's newsletter today: www.katyregnery.com!

www.ingramcontent.com/pod-product-compliance
Lightning Source LLC
Chambersburg PA
CBHW060435180626
46817CB00007B/2822